THE HIDDEN ONES

THE HIDDEN ONES

dave ring

Queer Space

New Orleans

Published in the United States of America and United Kingdom by
Queer Space
A Rebel Satori Imprint
www.rebelsatoripress.com

Paperback ISBN: 978-1-60864-176-5
Ebook ISBN: 978-1-60864-177-2
Library of Congress Control Number: 2021943225

 sat askew on a fine chair at tea amidst Miss Nora Sloe and her friends, limp-wristed and droll, saying anything and everything to ensure that she found me an amiably foppish companion. Practically a muppet. Afternoon tea at the Shelbourne meant a ceaseless army of dainty sandwiches, a veritable deluge of pointless chatter, and enough clinking of porcelain to wake the dead. It was a torment to my wrecked head and carried on long enough to make me doubt my own immortality. Nora controlled the room from a beige settee, clearly in her element, riding whatever wave of notoriety powered the post-collegiate Anglo-Irish 20-something set. The half of the room that wasn't staring at me looked at her out of the corner of their eyes.

The ordeal felt endlessly burdensome, especially the day after a funeral, but one does what is necessary to maintain the favor of a key dairy magnate's favorite daughter. Particularly when it only required that which came naturally: wielding a keen sense of disdain and making sure her serfs knew their place. My neighbors had learnt their lesson, and now spent more time on their phones than speaking.

Nora nattered on about fabric choices while I punished myself with a particularly difficult sudoku. "Baird, darling, what do you think of the damask? I was thinking of doing up the back of the car with some softer detailing. Leather is so—so—*stodgy*, you know?"

I wrinkled my nose at a column that refused to work itself out. The state I was in. "Oh poppet, the color is gorgeous, but wouldn't you have concerns about the integrity of the silk." Not a question. I left unsaid that leather remained rather more classic than stodgy.

"I suppose you have a point." Nora bit her lip and twisted brown hair between her fingers. Though the *words* she used were insufferable, her voice itself had a marvelously supple quality; I'd garnered my introduction to her through an "accidental" duet in a hotel lobby several months back. It made even the trite rubbish typically escaping her lips completely bearable.

"Something to ponder. But tell me more about that gala you're planning. For the wee children."

Nora clapped her hands in delight and began spouting off the courses she'd be serving. Everything felt so trivial, knowing that Glenn was dead. Even more than usual.

I ignored the unsilenced sound of a photo taken on a mobile phone. It came with the territory. Five hundred quid a plate. Not that I should talk. In my heyday, I'd probably snorted cocaine costing as much to while away a lazy Sunday afternoon. And really, this couldn't be as bad as the carry on I'd once been forced to blather on about when I first began cultivating Nora's affection. I'd been ridden with a coyness that curdled my own stomach until I realized that it wasn't necessary. I just needed to show a bit of interest in her projects to turn her a little locomotive that thrived on curiosity and compliments. After that it felt much less unpleasant having these tea parties.

And fair play to her. Nora possessed a certain steel; only someone very self-possessed can manage a conversation with one of my people without devolving into a simpering mess.

he night before, during a perfect June evening at St. Stephen's Green, nine o'clock at night and the sun still hanging over the horizon, a dead raven thumped into the grass beside my head, its wings crumpled and askew. A scrap of parchment protruded between the rictus-stricken halves of its closed beak.

I straightened its wings in a gesture of respect and pried the note from the bird's mouth. My heart sunk. The note bore a sigil made up of five horizontal lines struck through with a vertical slash. It meant that the Court of the Macha would be either welcoming a newborn or mourning one of their own, and no one had been born to the Macha since my sister, nearly a full ré ago—at least a thousand years. The note had no indication of a time, but there was no need. The

Macha always met at twilight.

I texted Kandace to cancel pints, but still made my way to the bar on the edge of Coombe that we'd arranged to meet, since it would suit this new purpose. The Court of the Macha held little truck with pretension and even less with cities. To manifest in Dublin, it would have to slink through half-built houses, via cul de sacs and unfinished rooftops. I had to meet it halfway, away from the horrid bustle of Grafton Street or Temple Bar. Dusk hovered on the edge of the sky, cutting into the last light of the balmy evening. I slipped into the beer garden behind my destination, the air thick with unusual sentiment, one that would soon send any punter who ventured out right back inside, their thoughts syrupy and strange.

But that is not to say the courtyard stood empty for long. Wherever we'd all been before Court, we met in an in-between place that defied common reality, and the Three who made up the Macha soon sat at a central table. Family, all of them, to my ever-present dismay. My aunt, always the drabbest of them, her dyed tawny locks tucked into a dirty grey hood, feet shod for riding and legs snug in black denim. She alone of the Three met my eye, although I can't say I liked what I saw there. Maeve, dear sister, held her attention determinedly over my shoulder. She wore business attire, a pantsuit even. She clearly hadn't called up this court. Granddame likely didn't ignore me on purpose, but had lost herself in preparations, perhaps to looking out for any unwelcome visitors. I could see why—we were so unlike to manifest in the city that another court may come calling to try and discover the purpose. Granddame had dressed in typical trousers and linens; she might have come right from the stable with Fea.

I considered skulking at the back, but bit the bitter seed and sat with Tadgh, another one who wouldn't look at me, for rather greater cause than Maeve. His long blonde hair had been hidden under a cap. Anger made the planes of his face tight against his cheekbones. He kept his eyes on the Three, the picture of obedience, but the surface of him roiled. Fury spun from sugar. My doing—I hadn't seen him in months. My consort. What a farce.

Others of the court filed in, most with pints in hand. I wasn't the only one who'd manifested beside a pub. I hadn't been among this many of the tuath for a long time. There were at least twenty of us. I didn't see Glenn, but Ciara lurked in the back where I'd wanted to stand. Someone brought the Three a tray of hot whiskies. I noted those who acknowledged me and those who shifted or looked away.

At some point I recalled that I should ask who we'd lost, but just then Granddame sipped at her whisky and cleared her throat. Those few who had been murmuring to themselves quieted, until the only noise came from passing cars on the other side of the courtyard wall and the muffled chatter of folks inside the pub. Granddame flexed her will, making the air even thicker with the presence of the tuath, and that noise dimmed. As if I wasn't in a beer garden at all, but instead the summit of a twilit hilltop, air sweet with loam and wilderness: the court had manifested in full.

Granddame didn't greet us further. The Three stood, as one, to our eyes each stretched much taller than the five odd feet they'd been moments ago. This seemed odd to me only when I looked at Maeve—I'd known her much longer as my sister than as one of the Three. Now her countenance bristled with vitality; it surrounded me like a cruel handshake.

"A breath caught betwixt singing and crying—" the Three spoke in unison, an incantation for the dead. The words had a timbre much deeper than any of the three typically possessed, and it became difficult to actually hear them. I registered the sound more through resonance and memory rather than comprehension. These syllables were dusky with the sound of thousands of feathers buffeting air, wind rushing through ears on a night in the saddle, the echoing unsound of mortality.

The call snaked its way inside of me and I closed my eyes while it took up residence in my gut. It walloped me with an inchoate sorrow. I waited for the warmth to come after, the balm to this loss: because isn't it true that tuath never really die? The light of them, their saol, comes back. And though we have the sting of their lost company, their essence is still a part of us all.

But it didn't come; my pulse quickened. My eyes fluttered open. I wasn't the only one—Ciara and I shared a glance of confusion, then turned to the Three. Their faces betrayed nothing. When the saol should have spread overhead like a mist and then slid into us all like sugar into a teacup, nothing happened. The loss of it under over us like a pall, and I wondered if this was how mortal folks felt when they lost someone.

Tadhg saw me and his lip twitched. "Who?" I asked quietly, even as not knowing made me angry at myself. Made me terrified at who Tadhg would name.

"Glenn," he mouthed back, barely words.

Glenn. All of us here were some sort of kin, but Glenn had been more than that. There'd been a time, when he'd been wooing Fea, that he'd almost been like a father. He'd race her across the horizon like a young fool, coming home to tell us stories and make us meals of rhubarb and fennel, wild mushrooms and rabbit. A far sight better than our real father. And now he was dead.

My eyes were hot with tears. Tadgh took pity on me and held my arm.

The Three spoke in harmony again, a dismissal.

When the trio of unearthly lips ceased to speak, the power that made them the Three fell away from their combined aspects one by one. Maeve was first to weaken, and Aunt Fea moments later. Granddame held her aspect for a full minute after, her eyes white with cataracts and yet still able to convey the terrible breadth of her sight. She subsided into her own form with a graceful exhale instead of the exhausted shaking of the others, making her mastery quite clear to any who might think she was in anything less than the prime of her power.

Granddame and Maeve turned to leave immediately. It

seemed there would be no other court business. I stood, voice caught in my throat. Surely someone would ask them what was wrong.

I would have spoken, I nearly would have yelled, but Fea appeared. One of her hands rested on Tadhg's shoulder, the other on mine.

I didn't yell, even though I wanted to. "That's it? You're saying nothing at all?"

Fea ignored my question. "Tadhg, I'm sorry to intrude, but I must beg a moment with Baird."

My consort regarded her with tired calculation. Fea had always been the least likely to discourage me from my sundry past times, but she was also one of the few elders I was prone to listen to. He rose to his feet. No matter how long we were together, I always forgot that he had a few inches on my six feet—he was usually slouching.

"Perhaps you'll join the two of us for a pint when you're done with him, Fea? It's been ages since we've had a proper chat," Tadgh said, full of brittle cheer. I frowned at him. He could join her for tea twice daily and still tend to his own matters.

"Oh pet, I'd love to, I would. But not this eve, I'm afraid. Would you call over to me during the week instead?" Fea asked.

An awkward pause. We all refused to look each other in the eye.

I caught Tadhg's attention. "I'll meet you in the Central Hotel as soon as we've finished?"

His fire subsided. He fluttered a hand at me to acquiesce, tying his cardigan tighter around him, and drifted over to the other departing tuath.

"When did you learn about Glenn?" I asked.

"Baird, I'm running out of smokescreen." Fea's voice hissed like a tire. "You are a bloody expense report that I have more and more difficulty explaining. Have you even *talked* to the Sloes lately?"

I'd hardly even thought of them, but I knew the bollocking I'd get if I said that. Before I stuttered out a response, she gripped my chin with calfskin gloves, tight enough to hurt. "Shut your hole. Get your shit together, Baird. I love you like my own heart, but if you don't put aside your faffing about, you're going to be contemplating those West Cork skylines you have so little patience for."

"The Sloes are well in hand. There have just been some…" I honestly didn't have any excuses. "Some distractions."

"That's not what your sister says. Maeve has suggested that you might be better utilized at home. Get it together."

I blinked at her. Fea had the ability to make me feel like a child in a way no one else could.

"Do you understand?" She still hadn't let go of my chin. It was exactly like my youth.

"Yes." The word caught in my throat as I spoke, too close to a sob for my liking. "But Glenn—"

"No, love. I can't think about that right now." Fea let go and pecked me on the cheek. "Go sort out things with Tadhg. Or at least appease him for the next while so you can get this done. I don't need you distracted. And—" Fea cut herself off, doubting herself.

"What? What a Riven-poxing load of—"

"Don't cuss at me, you langer. Because he loves you. *Actually* loves you."

I closed my eyes, but when I opened them, Fea still stood there. "I know," I said. "I know. I just wish I could make that mean more to me these days."

"Oh, Baird. I wish that—"

It appeared to be my turn to cut her off now. "No, Fea, don't. You know that even if Granddame or Tadhg's court or *Tadhg* would accept it, he would never suffer that disgrace. He would rather … anything else." I shrugged. "So we go on."

Fea's lips fell into a displeased line. We parted without goodbyes. The Library Bar at the Central Hotel was not far from where the Macha had manifested. I found Tadhg slouched in an armchair, drinking tea with a newspaper, in the middle of the half-full room. I leaned against the doorframe to watch him for a minute. Like any room with one of the tuath within it, the common folk there found themselves subconsciously drawn to him. Two servers stopped to tidy the sugar bowl on his table, staring at him through their eyelashes. A group of students nearby kept trailing off in the middle of their sentences to moon after him.

But after a few moments, the young fellow behind the bar stared at me instead, because there were now two tuath in his establishment. I brought two pints over to the table as a peace offering. Tadhg looked up with a wry smile and glanced around him, clearly aware of the attention. It felt like sly commentary; his consort was the only thing in the room that did not revolve around him. Although my presence in the middle of this whirlpool of attention had a drastic effect—now everyone found themselves regarding us without the slightest bit of self-awareness.

I could never find the right thing to say in these moments. I wanted to shout at him about all the ways that I was hurting, but it shouldn't really be about me. I'd already fucked things up to the point of misery.

"I can't believe he's gone. How—"

"Shut up, Baird."

Being wrong just felt so shitty, I had to barrel on. "I can't say you've been pleased with me, dear heart. And I'm sorry for that." It was the best I could think of.

Tadhg's irises were icy blue lasers. "As usual, you apologize for my displeasure rather than your behavior. Baird, you've been gone for months. How many I'm not even sure now, is it seven?"

"No more than six, really, I'm sure of it."

He looked at me.

I looked away. "I have obligations, Tadhg. For the Court. You know that. I suppose I should call more."

His laugh could cut glass.

"Tadhg, I'm sorry, I—"

"*No*, Baird. Just, just—*no*. I have had more of you being sorry than I know what to do with. If I'd known then what

11

I know now, I'd have thought twice about promising you *forever*, I'll tell you that."

The room's denizens began to take on the character of his speech, their lips curling in dismay at the anger building between us.

His voice broke a bit. "Baird, what sort of coward are you? Just say it should be sundered and be done with me." His fury never lasted long. This wouldn't end well.

He stood; I grabbed his hand. Despite it all, our hands always fit together so well.

He pulled away and took a deep breath, his eyes glistening. He bent down quickly and kissed my forehead. One onlooker gasped, probably struck dumb with the enthralling beauty of us.

"Come home when you can. We'll talk then." Swallowed tears made his voice low and heavy. "Glen left a note."

I let him go. My unused words circled in my head, pointless and inconsequential as toy trains.

After Tadgh left, those words swirled in my head. A note. Glenn had killed himself? I couldn't believe it.

My phone shook in my pocket.

A text from Kandace: *At Hogans by the window. I saw you walk by with the pretty boy. Come in for a gargle when you've finished rubbing his heart against a cheese grater.*

t was bad, eh?" Kandace's dark brown skin and headwrap stuck out like a sore thumb in the otherwise all-white room. But once she opened her mouth, her accent was pure Northside Dublin, rough and tumble around the edges.

I nodded.

She caught the bartender's eyes, tore them off me really, and got us a pint. Kandace had a good eye for when to ask questions and when to let silence speak for itself. She was young, nothing on my years, but still cocky. Insightful. A mystery still, in a lot of ways. She wasn't tuath, she was something else entirely, though she refused to explain whenever I tried to pry. I'd thought it had to do with the three lines scarred onto her cheeks, but when I asked, she'd rolled her eyes at that one. "It's a traditional family thing, Baird. Google it before you say anything else dumb."

One pint became two, then dinner. More than once I opened my mouth to say something about Tadg or Glenn, but I hadn't found the words yet. Kandace went outside for a smoke, after, so I watched an aul fella with a guitar settle into the snug beside us. Two women joined him—sisters I thought at first, until they had a quick snog when the old man went to the toilet. Your one had a bodhrán, the other a fiddle. Kandace returned and there was laughing and shouting—of course she knew them. It didn't take long for the fiddler to ask her to sing something. Kandace asked me if I minded with a raised eyebrow. I shrugged. Of course not. She spoke a moment, introducing the tune. The old song rose like a flag—She Moved Through the Fair—and her voice promptly haunted every single punter in that place into a silence so strong they almost stopped breathing. She met my eye again as it wound up. I nodded and ordered us two more pints. We could be here awhile. It reminded me of the night we met. Kandace knew immediately that I was *more than*, in some way. We'd drank Jameson long into the night. I learned her story, born in Ireland to Nubian Sudanese parents before the Celtic Tiger. We danced around much of the more mysterious details of our lives, while still tacitly acknowledging their existence. Since then, I've told her much more of my Court, and she knows well my long history with Tadhg.

Kandace begged off after the second song and came back to our table. But when she checked her phone, she winced.

"Gotta go?"

"I have a *paying* gig on Dame Street now, believe it or not. Sorry pet."

She left me with a belly full of venison and Jameson. But I wasn't ready to slide into grief; I needed more drink. I slid into one pub and then the next, more whisky and then singing. Both made me less distracting and more charming: punters were less put off being struck dumb by a man's voice than they were by the sheer sight of him.

My feet took me to a selection of dives and bars, finishing in that stable of narcissists on George's Street where we were prone to have the odd ironic cocktail. The admiration wasn't real, but for now it would do. Until it didn't.

 got home without too many bruises, but that seemed to be the only positive thing I could say about my behavior when I woke up the next morning. I'd managed to undress the top half of me, but I actually fell out of bed upon waking due to my trousers still being attached to my ankles. Hardly my worst moment, but the headache certainly made it feel like it until the boy came up with some coffee.

The knock on the door came too early for the coffee so I thought about snarling. Instead, I glanced at my phone. Four texts from Kandace, long after I'd made it into drunken dreamland.

1:12am: *Where you at Baird? Gig finished and I'm feeling reckless.*

1:15am: *I tried Sorcha's but she's already asleep and snoring like a dog*

1:35am: *don't tell me you went home*

2:02am: *fuck you baird you're buying me breakfast tomorrow*

Was I wearing pants? Yes. I got up and opened the door. Kandace *and* the boy with the coffee. I ignored Kandace's face to take the cup and saucer from him. "Actually, a pot of coffee will do. And two full breakfasts. And tea. Thanks."

"And a croissant, cheers," Kandance said to his back as she entered; the boy nodded and left.

Kandace hurled herself onto the bed, boots laced to her

knees and all. I tut tutted from my spot by the door and sipped at the foam of my cup, tastefully made into some frothy, frond-like shape. She folded the duvet back over herself to leave the twisted sheets and things exposed. Her big hoop earrings jutted out at odd angles from the pillows.

"How's Sorcha?" I asked. It was perfunctory but at least I asked.

Kandace just rolled her eyes at me. "She is great. Delicious, really. How's *Tadhg*, you twat?"

I shrugged. "I don't know what I'm doing."

Kandace sat up immediately. "What happened?" Her expression went south. "Did something terrible happen?"

"No, not exactly," I said, then thought about Glenn. "Well, sort of." The words felt less heavy today. But my grief should be, some semblance of mourning, I only had numbness. I told her about the meeting, most of it anyway. I may have made myself sound better in that interaction with Fea.

"Fuck, Baird. I'm so sorry." I reckon Kandace would have whistled if she knew how. "Fuck," she said again.

"Yeah."

"So, are you gonna go run shit before Auntie comes down hard on you?"

I sigh. "I'll visit the younger Sloe later today. So that will be that."

"Well, that'll be the family; off your tits, right?" Kandace laid her head back down on the pillow, pulled the duvet close again. "Wait," she said. "Does that mean you'll be bound for the country for awhile again?"

"I'd like to spend some time on the hills there. It seems the best way to remember him. See as he's not...back with us. And besides, Tadhg—"

Someone knocked on the door. Letting the boy bustle about setting up our trays and taking off the silver lids and whatnot gave me a moment to prepare myself. I pulled the desk chair over and Kandace slid to the edge of the bed. She took the puddings from my plate and slid over her fatty bacon to mine without even asking. We both ignored our roast tomato.

"I'm still mad you went home last night."

"Not like you can match pints with me anyway."

The pillow bounced off my face and into my plate before I knew it, beans and egg splattering everywhere, my eyes included. Kandace was laughing and on her knees with one of the cloth napkins before I even had a chance to curse at her.

"Get the fuck out of Dublin, Baird," she said from the ground. "You're no fun when you're having marital strife."

I tried to gather my words, but I had no wry rejoinder, so instead I nodded.

"And take a shower," Kandace said. "You fecking reek."

knew that I couldn't ignore an inevitable return for much longer. Fea would be satisfied with Nora's renewed decisions in the market, but no satisfaction would have her forgive me this hotel bill if I stayed here much longer without an heiress to work over.

So, coffee vanquished, and after a wash, I readied myself to leave the city. I packed terribly, considering how much traveling I did, but I compensated by always carrying a much bigger suitcase than any particular trip really warranted so that when it was over I could just feck it all in without paying much attention. All the extra things I'd bought over the last couple months when my stay became longer and longer—runners I'd worn once, an endless number of jumpers, a waistcoat that didn't actually fit—were thrown into a pile by the bin. I'd put a note saying that they should donate it, but I wouldn't be surprised if the room service didn't take my fancy rags for themselves.

My driver handled her Traction Avant like a pro, one begloved hand constantly toying with her pearls. Jimmy knew I didn't mind whatever played on the radio, so we listened to NPR podcasts from America the whole drive, one after another, with just a tiny break in the middle for a bit of Nina Simone. It was quite nice really and settled me into a quieter version of myself.

There's something quite daredevilish about driving even moderately fast on these roads. To call them roads was kind in some places, and really, this close to the Sheep's Head

Peninsula they'd be more often used by cows than cars in some places, although luckily Jimmy had no need for unexpected maneuvers.

A feeling comes over me whenever I come home. The old ones said it's the land speaking to you, which might be true. If I had to say, it's like the breeze had a particular taste to it and the sunlight felt different on my skin. From the moment we arrived until the long driveway leading up to the actual house, I wondered why it was that I spend so much time away from here. Who in their right mind would want to not feel this way, when all they need to do in order to feel alive was come home?

Jimmy opened the car door with a bow somewhere between debonair and demure. The twinkle in her eye was all Dublin git. I slipped a hundred quid note into her hand while I air-kissed her glove. I don't think we exchanged more than a few words the whole trip, but her presence was a balm. She and the car departed presently.

As I neared the house, I savored the feeling of home with a ferocity that seemed to be asking for trouble, as if I'd resigned myself to ruining whatever moments came next. But my hand rested on the doorknob, unable to open the damn thing. It almost irritated me that Jimmy had left so efficiently—I could never have drawn out this moment if I'd known her eyes were on me.

A flash of movement on the other side of the frosted glass preceded Cicely, in her casual apron, washcloth in hand. She was far too precise to ever really look surprised.

"Master Baird, welcome home," she said, setting down the bucket in her other hand.

"Madam Cicely. Thank you, hello. Is Master Tadhg in residence?" I was being polite, Tadgh had far too large a sense of duty to be anything other than in residence. The sense of obligation that rose up in me made me frown.

"I beg pardon, Master Baird."

I started. "Oh, no, Cicely. Not you, I was caught up in my own head just there. Say that again?"

"Master Tadhg is taking tea with your sister and a gentleman named Mister Meadows. Shall I announce you?" Cicely eyed me warily, hand beginning to tug at her kerchiefed red hair. Meadows was a local. Business meeting? Ciceley was clearly not dressed for any sort of announcing. I'd say she'd thought she had time to do some cleaning while they handled whatever they were discussing.

I shook my head.

She nodded. "Leave your bag by the door there, Master Baird, and go freshen up. I'll have your things brought up."

I spent a moment in the jacks splashing water on my face, discarded half my clothes. I left my shirt and waistcoat on the floor and sauntered into the parlour with my belt half undone and vest untucked.

The arrangement of the three of them in the parlour wasn't unquaint. Maeve had dressed for entertaining in a glossy black frock and metallic heels, while Tadhg presented himself like a rural dandy in heather pinstripes and linen. Their companion, this Mister Meadows, could only be coarse by comparison. He wore a respectable brown jacket over his shirt and denim, but he couldn't have looked more out of place in my parlour, uncouth against its lacquered lines and opulent patterns. Not that I'd had anything to do with it—before Tadgh moved onto the estate most of the furniture had been covered with dropcloths and stacked in boxes. In any case, Maeve and Tadhg's body language conveyed languid deferment to his social authority. All of Maeve's lines pointed at him and her half-lidded gaze was a force unto itself. Tadhg had seated himself on a slightly lower chair to undercompensate for his height, and held a tray of biscuits in his hand as if he were ready to proffer one to Meadows at the first inkling he was in need of a Milano.

Meadows noticed me first, and by his pursed lipshe hadn't the slightest idea who I was, which put the childish edge of a sneer on my face. I wished I'd walked in wearing only my shorts. Maeve caught on quick though and arched her elegant eyebrow. "Michael, have you met my older brother, Baird? He mostly handles the Dublin accounts. Baird, this is Michael Meadows, here to fill us in on the fall yields."

I shook the man's hand and did how-do-you-dos as I settled beside him, close enough that I could feel the warmth of him. He smelled like sweat and summer and fresh cut grass. My smile veered closer to a leer than my consort and sister would approve. "Well now, we haven't met before, but I'm certainly familiar with your father's reputation. Strong stock you come from, the Meadows." I slapped his thigh with a grin and leaned back into the couch. I plucked a cookie from Tadhg's tray without looking at him and shoved it into my face, crumbs falling everywhere.

"What do you think of my family's hospitality? Have they given you the big house treatment?"

Maeve scowled and Tadhg's smile became impossibly brittle.

Meadows clearly didn't know how to answer. This many tuath together must be making his head thick, and with my entrance, the atmosphere had become toxic. "You—you must be tired after your trip, perhaps I should go?" He looked uncertainly at my partner.

Meadows was no warrior. It wasn't difficult to make the man look like a boy in my shadow. I knew my looks had none of the fairness of Maeve and Tadhg—where they were otherworldly and graceful, I'd been hewn of stronger bones. If there was beauty in my visage it was in my solidity, the years that settled into the sun-flecked crows' feet at the corners of my eyes. It irked me that even as I chafed at my ties to Tadgh these days it took so little for me to start acting the jealous husband. I didn't need to see his tired frown to know that I was being stupid. Meadows hadn't come here for a pissing contest. Tadhg hadn't really planned on seducing him—he wasn't even acting the part. He did his duty for the Macha, making this local businessman feel at home in the face of our wealth, at least enough that he might feel like he held the upper hand. My little display of virility was just fucking it up.

"Forgive me. The road puts me out of sorts. Stay. Have a

biscuit." I borrowed the tray from Tadgh. Still hadn't looked him in the eye. Meadows took a Milano. "They're from America, good stuff. Say haven't I seen you at Roche's with Ol' Red? I think I may actually owe you a pint. Bad form, owing a man a pint. Least I can do is give you a few biscuits." My banter found easy purchase—everyone in the area drank at Roche's and knew the owner.

Meadows and I kept it going for a bit until Tadhg stepped in to rein the conversation back to where he wanted it. On the way to business ventures, he went through easy topics— the weather, an errant sheep that had stopped up the road for hours last Sunday after church. Although that may have been a brief misstep since any local would know that no one from this house ever found themselves in church on the Lord's day. Maeve kept on playing the coquette, although now more restrained since her perhaps protective brother was in the room. I think it pushed Meadows' buttons, the married bastard.

When it seemed clear my damage had been mended, I excused myself and headed out the back to the promontory. The spit of land jutted just wide enough to bear its rocks and some heather, but it held enough heft for the curve of land to make its way around a tiny little cove of our own. And just where the cove began to fold back into the line of the promontory, a seat had been carved into the rock, a foot or two wider than two people would need to sit side by side. The same rock where Tadhg and I had promised ourselves to each other, just wearing our skins, speaking oaths profound to the Macha and sacred to the Muir, the strongest we could come up with. Anything to keep our courts from war.

Our story had many of the hallmarks of a ballad. The songs were written. Plenty had sung them. But having lived it, being called a hero in such romantic songs, it still struck me as if they must be singing of someone else. Especially since invariably Tadgh or I became a maiden in recent renditions. Tadhg's beauty meant he was usually the one cast as the damsel, but since he'd been the one who fought Fea for my hand, the details that followed were usually far from what truly happened.

On a cold summer's morn'
By the wild of the sea
Came the champion of the Macha
And from the Muir there was he

As they stood against the seafoam
The skies wept and raged
Would this mean freedom
Or a great people caged

The Muir's warrior was clad
In naught but love's new union
He faced the earth-queen maiden
And offered her communion

Then the Muir pointed out his love

It was ever so florid. And didn't initially rhyme in any language we bothered speaking anymore, so it always ended up sort of jammed into any old measure. It had a certain cadence in the modern Irish that wasn't displeasing, and most versions were overly obsessed with when Tadhg managed to unseat Fea from her horse while he fought on foot—everyone knew that no tuath of the Macha could be separated from their footing on land or horse while the earth still gave us her favor. But of course, Tadhg had just been grafted to the Macha by our oaths, so he surprised her. Dumb luck, but we'd counted on it. And in the aftermath, we'd made an alliance between our peoples, a true comhar based on love and idealistic vows.

Now, as I approached the sea chair, the waves rose in intensity, slapping harder against the rocks. I would not be the fool who thought the sea did not know more of me than I told it, but damned if I would let it begrudge me deeds undone. I threw the rest of my clothes to the ground and lowered myself into the water without flinching, the chill shrinking my balls and raising up gooseflesh across every inch of my skin.

The Macha's adage would hold true while I clung to the rock of the chair, but I would also claim the rights of my bonds to Tadhg as my own until they were broken, so I pushed away from the rock and dove out between the two outcroppings of stone that marked the entrance to my little cove. The Atlantic toyed with me, pulled and pushed at my limbs, but I rode it, reminded it to respect me yet. It would not caress me, or carry me on its back like a child of the Muir, but it would gentle to my touch long enough to not to dash me against the rocks.

When I wearied, I swam back through the cove's guardian pillars and clambered up the rock to one of my sun spots to dry out. I laid there for long minutes, baking in the last of the day's rays. It was odd to think that if Tadhg and I chose to break our vows through mutual choice or my disreputable actions, then I would never swim in Eire's waters again.

 didn't bother dressing when I went back inside. Meadows would be long gone and Cicely should be gone for the day. My thoughts grew reckless. I went upstairs.

I slid into his room—our room— found it dark, the shades drawn. My eyes were slow to adjust after staring at the sunset, so when the shadows parted to reveal Tadhg sitting upright on the edge of the bed, waiting for me, I nearly jumped.

His stare was intense, but as I read further into it, hungry too. I buried my half-hearted explanations and pushed him back on the bed. He licked the sea from my skin and replaced it with sweat. I tore at his lower lip with biting kisses, ground his nipples between my fingers. Usually Tadhg was a selfish fuck, but for some reason he was keen on pleasing me. It caught me off guard. It made a beast of me. We came together and finished with shouting and half numb limbs and exhausted smiles.

This love had once stopped an army.

He fell asleep easily, face tucked into the crook of my arm and leg half over mine. My mind raced in the darkness. I focused on the cooling beads of sweat that dripped slowly down the side of my face. It should have been perfect, but it wasn't. And I didn't have the stones to admit it to him.

When I decided that dawn lurked on the other side of those thick curtains, I slid out of the sheets. I dressed in runners and gym shorts, before asking Cicely in the kitchen to call Jimmy. She nodded to me with a small frown that I decided not to mind.

The hills between our estates had long belonged to the Macha. Before roads and automobiles, Glenn had taught Maeve and I to ride across them on stocky storm grey ponies. It was hard to pass a fence or a hillock, knowing that it was the place that Maeve had almost beaten the life from me for ruining her prize blade, or that was the tree we'd hid behind as we'd pretended not to watch Glenn and Fea have a quick snog in the underbrush.

Maeve's complex of buildings had been built further up the coast, a good hour's walk, but not too long of a run. By the time I got there, my heart felt heavy, I was sweating something furious, and my head was so hot that it steamed.

Her body man met me inside the entrance by the stable. Apparently, this morning she had a lesson with her tai chi instructor. Her butler thought to bring me to the parlour but noted my general swampiness.

"The lady usually enjoys a stint in the steam room after her sessions with Sifu Anna. Perhaps I can escort you there while you wait?" His posh London accent was precisely deferential. I thought about giving him trouble just to watch that thin mustache of his quiver, but the steam room sounded lovely.

I let the man escort me back outside towards her spa suite before I asked his name and received a terse, "St. Claire, sir, Benjamin." At first, his tone piqued me but it occurred to me that I'd likely asked him that before. Maeve's grounds were predictably beautiful. The paths were laid with tiny white stones, the ground on either side mottled with moss and rock and purple heather. She and her instructor's silhouettes were visible up on the hill, and even at a glance they were poised in very graceful shapes.

The spa had been set up like its own villa. White stone, warm wood and glass. Floors made from blush marble shot through with gold. The layout opened into the changing area, with half-private cubbies for disrobing, stacks of plush white towels and a shower hidden behind a translucent white pane of glass. Massage tables. Potted bamboo. More serenity than I knew what to do with. It made me slightly nauseated.

A cold shower, a lovely towel and a further disapproving look from St. Claire saw me into the steamroom. It was difficult to stop myself from toying with him further, but I had to admit that the allure was largely due to the fact that he hadn't the slightest interest in my charms. He obviously bore the mark of the raven just as Cicely did. How tiresome to interact with common folk who didn't bend to my will. It was all for the best, I suppose. I wouldn't want any bold tuath ordering Cicely around.

Eucalyptus began to permeate the room. My lungs tingled pleasantly, and I sat in the dim light with my eyes closed. At one point when I opened them, Maeve sat there beside me, identical fluffy towel wrapped around her waist, chest still heaving from her exertions. Neither of us felt the need to talk right away.

But the silence couldn't last forever. "Are you coming or going, brother?"

I thought about Jimmy, already driving back from the city to fetch me. "I'm hardly a homebody, Maeve."

"This will not end well," she said.

"I *do* still love him," I said. This was not enough, and we both knew it.

Silence, until: "If you break your vows, the alliance would still stand." Perhaps because she was talking now of Court business, but it seemed as though her voice had dropped in pitch. My ribs shook.

I exhaled sharply, inhaling more eucalyptus. It had begun to burn a bit. "That is comforting. I just—"

"That doesn't mean that Granddame won't have to render judgement." I think concern hid beneath her censure, but I didn't want to pretend I understood all the changes that had come to her since she became part of the Macha.

I felt my heart go hard, and with it my voice. "So be it."

I waited, but she said nothing. Had I made a decision? It didn't feel like I had. "Put me to work with the Gaita," I suggested. "Some inter-Court diplomacy."

Maeve snorted and scratched her tit. I found myself mimicking her in unintentional sympathetic body language until I caught myself. "After that dinner party? It seems hardly wise. No, that's a snarl I can't risk you in. And I've already handled it. Sorry, brother. You might need to deal with the—"

"I need you to send me away. To think. If I must do Court work to loosen your purse-strings, I'll do it." My fists clenched.

Maeve stood up and leaned against the wall. "Baird, honestly, if you didn't squander every coin, every pound, and now every euro you ever found in your possession, you wouldn't need to come plucking at our apron whenever you found yourself brooding and skint."

"I *earn* my *keep*, dear sister. Don't forget that."

Maeve laughed cruelly. "With what? Your little social missions, like with the Sloes? You and your stodgy complaints."

I rocked back a bit. But Maeve wasn't done.

"Poor *Nora*, that girl. Having to listen to you prattling on about interior design. Honestly, couldn't you learn something about the stock market so that you have something sparkling to add to the conversation? The woman is a *doctor of economic theory*, and you've managed to alienate her to the point that she only feels comfortable talking with you about inane fabric choices."

"Oh, come now Maeve, let's not even pretend that she has the willpower to—"

"Stop. I've *marked* her, Baird. She's as much mine as Benjamin."

I practically felt capillaries bursting in my cheeks. I was mortified. Pure scarlet.

"You've been played, *dear brother*. By yourself. You managed to ruin a pity assignment. If Granddame and I had our way, you'd be tucked away here at home for the rest of the ré where you can't spend the Court's money so readily."

I would have lashed back at her—I had the barbs ready on my tongue—but she started back up again. "We've business in Lough Derravaragh you can attend to. Fea is there as well. For some reason she's requested your presence. If you want to try and think of something besides your own miseries for once, ask her of her troubles. She's certainly the reason you're not in more of your own."

Maeve left in a whoosh of steam as the door slammed behind her.

I swore at her, then sat on the bench for awhile longer, trying to collect myself. How dare she make me look like a fool? Who else knew? Pushing my towel aside, I rubbed one out on her pristine tiles before I left, imagining the hungry mouth of St. Clair.

The fleeting pleasure and the sense of childishness that followed burned nearly as much as the shame I'd hoped to abjure. By the time I got my clothes back, they smelled like fresh air and Daz. I dressed quickly. St. Clair regarded me with nearly no expression, but I didn't need hundreds of years of experience to register his low opinion of me.

Lough Derravaragh wasn't quite *on the way* but it was better than here.

ack at the estate, I changed into slacks and Arran wool from my second closet on the ground floor—the day had gotten chill. Wheels on gravel alerted me to my ride. I gave Jimmy a half wave and a quick gesture at my lack of appropriate travel wear. She acknowledged me with a slight tilt to her chin. As I got closer to the door, it was opened by the ever-efficient Cicely. I pointedly didn't look around for Tadhg; safe to say that he would be upstairs fuming until I left.

Cicely would have already put my bags into the car. Steps out of the house, I did an about face and looked up at the window. He was there all right. Blonde tresses shielding his eyes, cheek pressed to the hard glass like a photograph of a ghost. I tore back inside and took the steps two at a time, the door open before I remembered touching the doorknob, and I kissed him so hard our teeth mashed together. I held the back of his head and cradled him to my chest, rocking back and forth while he shook with tears.

"Oh, my love," I said over and over until I practically hummed it. "My love."

If only I could love him so easily at that moment always.

I didn't cry until Jimmy closed the door to the car with a practiced hand. I have always been told, by Maeve and Tadgh especially, that I cry with unfair beauty. Tears fell from my eyes in glistening rivulets. I considered it fair turn around that the brute should have easy tears while both their more genteel looks should cry with blotches and sobs.

Jimmy let me sit with myself for a number of miles before she silently passed me an embroidered handkerchief, then hit play on the stereo. We travelled without words, just the entire Belle & Sebastian back catalogue.

I found Fea in a pub in Mullingar. Fea had a bundle from the chipper around the corner and a Guinness in front of her; the bartender was giving her plenty of space, but still staring distractedly at her from the end of the bar. The whole place probably only had five punters in it. She wore the same thing as when I'd last seen her days ago, hood down this time.

I sat beside her, asked for a Jameson. She didn't say anything right away, just turned slightly and lay her head on my shoulder. Not so different a pose from the one that Tadhg and I had been in hours ago, enough that my eyes watered a bit until I blinked them dry.

"How's the day finding you, my boy? And while I love seeing your face, give me one good reason for you being here." She punctuated her sentence by stuffing three mayonnaise-encrusted chips in her mouth. She hadn't moved her head so I couldn't read her face, but I was impressed as always at the way Fea combined affection with censure. I just hoped she didn't try to drink her pint from that angle.

I absent-mindedly patted her hair as I tried to come up with an explanation for her. She had it pinned back with an argent horse. The maker of the pin had crafted it with legs poised in motion, mane flying in the wind. "I don't have one, Auntie. All my reasons are awful."

Fea grunted a half-laugh and righted herself, jiggled around on her bar stool to face me more. "Well, you're in good company then. I take it Maeve sent you to attend me? That sly girl."

I wrinkled my brow at her. "More so than usual? She said you asked for me. Why, what's the story here?" I looked around the bar for effect. We were hardly at the epicenter of Court business. Only notable thing I could remember about Lough Derravaragh was that there'd been tell of a tuath court cursed into birds once; long before I was around though.

Fea opened her mouth to speak but seemed to have a hard time picking the right words to start out with. I could actually see the different thoughts flit across her broad face like birds. "I'm here to see your father, Baird."

My jaw dropped. "Why would you—"

"Cathal and I haven't been able to conceive either, Baird. That's the third pairing I've tried. The saol comes together and just … fades. So the Macha has, together, decided that

I should approach Cern, since he fathered the last of the Macha's young."

"Fathered is hardly the word I'd use for it. So, Maeve knows." I would have rolled my eyes if it had been something less serious. "But surely there've been others born after us. There must be. Birth and death for the Macha are..." I trailed off, miming a coin toss. But as I said it, I realized that I didn't really know of any, at least off the top of my head.

Fea was more sure. "Nope. Glenn fathered Tegan, shortly after you and Maeve, but the Boirinn claimed Tegan. They needed an heir, since the other young one they had was cursed."

"A curse," I echoed. "Who—"

"It doesn't matter," Fea said. "Maeve is still the baby since you beat her here by a few minutes. Glenn and I tried again, but it failed, like the others. And Glenn took it badly."

I shook my head. "It makes no sense."

"I know it doesn't—but it'd true."

None of it made sense. Not just the idea that Glenn would end his life. It still felt weird. Legend said that Granddame had given birth to Fea and my mother while riding on a horse, her sister riding beside her to catch them as they came out screaming. If the Macha couldn't make life, no one could. "But to go to Cern. After all this time. Has he even come down from the hill since we were born?"

Now she had a funny look on her face. "Well, he hasn't exactly come down. But we haven't been completely out of touch."

"Auntie Fea, have you been trysting with my sire and not telling me about it?" This was *shocking*. Truly shocking. My glibness felt like it would expire into hysteria at any moment.

Fea didn't even have the grace to blush once she had decided to use candour. "Not trysting, no. But after your mother died so soon after bearing you, I brought the news to him. Gave my token to the hill and met him there. And we took solace in each other that night, and when necessary thereafter. Cern is powerful, but do not forget that he is a Court of one. There are no other tuath who bear witness to the Ethliu but him."

"Foolish to bear young from the body," I said, for the hundredth time. "Tadhg was carried by a whale! Tegan gestated in a bloody stone."

"It's not our way, Baird. Your father understands that."

It still sat strangely with me. I'd never known my mother, and while they say that Maeve and I spent our first winter with Cern on his hill, I could not even describe his face. I have heard him called mystic, and strong in old ways even without the manifestation of Ethliu's aspect, but he'd not been part of the lives of tuath nor men for more than most of my many years.

My tongue had become bitter. "What need do you have of me then? Will I polish the furniture while you polish his knob?"

Immediately, Fea's fingers clutched at my chin. "Don't speak to me like that or I'll take you out to the yard and have a bash at you. And we both know which of us throws a better fist."

I tried to look daggers at her but likely only managed spoons. When she withdrew her hand, I rubbed at my face gingerly. Nothing I could say would make me less of an arse, so I didn't speak.

"Oh, get up, you fool. I'm dragging you up the damn hill. I'm almost as angry at Cern these days as I am with you, so I might as well inflict you on each other. I hope you brought practical footwear."

 had on brand new espadrilles, but they didn't last long. We'd barely set off from the road when I introduced one of them to a creek. Not one to cry over such things, I left them as an offering and continued with bare feet. My feet had been calloused by harder things than Cern's hill.

On the way, Fea talked. Apparently, what she mostly did with Cern was provide an audience of one for his rites. Ethliu had been big on the call and response, difficult to manage alone. And although there were no women of Ethliu to take on her full aspect as the court's tradition required, it seemed that over the years Cern had moved towards a state of androgyny that gave Ethliu a tenuous place to latch on to. This was strange to me—the bodies of the tuath were not fixed, though changes took centuries. Before joining the Three, and ascending into that matriarchal power, Maeve had spent half the last ré as a fey boy nearly as pretty as Tadhg. If Cern had wished to change his shape for Ethliu he could have, which made me believe that Cern was exactly as he wished to be.

Fea spoke of him with a distanced affection that gave me the sense that while she likely knew him the best of anyone else, there was still plenty to his mystery.

If we followed a particular trail, I couldn't see it. And while I had no particular gift for pathfinding, I do think that through sheer longevity most tuath have developed a fairly acute ability to see such where the usual gaze might not, so I reckoned it must be fairly well hidden. The air lay heavy with the scent of loam and rotting leaves. Fea led the way with confidence, though the places that she stopped to get her bearings had no similarities that I could tell.

The most noticeable thing about Cern's hill seemed to be the richness of its fauna. I would bet a small finger that he'd taken long steps to cultivate it. The hill bore the signs and spoor of many more creatures than would normally populate a Midlands wood—stoat and hare, fox and badger, squirrel and hedgehog. And the different birds on the wing were in the dozens. We didn't catch sight of them, but the wood never took on that sudden silence that fell upon the trespass of common folk, another thing I took for granted. As if the trees recognized that we were more ancient than themselves and made this known to their denizens.

Fea was easy to spend time with, on any day. As we walked, I felt Fea drawing on the Court of the Macha's massed saol, the power that kept us all together, that which made us Macha. Our numbers had always ebbed and flowed, but I felt the new thinness to our saol now that Glenn had left us, and his energy hadn't come back to us. Of my close family, we were like five beads embroidered on the same string, stretched across Eire: Granddame, cousin Ciara, Maeve, Fea and myself. With any luck, Fea would bring new life to the Macha.

I wouldn't mind a young one running around. I'd never been an uncle before.

When the path came to a cleft in a craggy rock ahead, it became clear to me that the hill's more primal nature would be asserting itself—there was no reason to move forward through such precarious territory but for the one path to the right that blocked by gnarled thickets (impenetrable I'm sure) and the way to the left tight with trees that had drunk up olde energies with the rainwater, and I knew that no matter my world-weary perceptions, if I ventured that way I would soon find myself back where I started. This crag wouldn't even be here if you looked at the hill from the sky.

When Fea turned a grey eye towards mine and stopped chattering midway through yet another yarn about my mother and her legendary pursuits, I knew that this must be where the hill made its choice—that is, whether to let travellers to its peak or do away with them. For this wasn't an unhungry hill. It had an appetite as real as any beast on its back.

We decided who would go first silently. I gestured Fea

ahead, reckoning that she'd gone up enough times before that she'd make it through with little ill effects. I hadn't failed to pick up on the fact that the hill's toll hadn't been in any of the stories that Fea had been telling as we hiked up, but neither did I feel particularly daunted.

The cleft in the rock was not a friendly path—to get through required careful footing and the leverage of strong arms against rock. And between one moment of looking down and the next of looking up, the triangle of open sky I had seen ahead had become mist. I lurched into it with a frisson of recognition at the most elementary parts of me sung out to the ancient powers there—

The path was still the same, but my perspective had dropped by about five feet. I felt like a traveller in someone else's skin. Fea came around the bend with a head of chestnut hair and the years fell away—I wasn't riding just anyone's memory—this was my own. My disembodied heart contracted painfully when a raven-haired woman appeared and swooped in to pick me up.

I felt my infant thoughts there beside my own, but they were simple and easily satiated. My young self must have felt some semblance of the stowaway adult tucked into his head, because he started to fret at my mother's face and made petty mewling noises. She responded by tucking his head into her hair, and I found myself wishing I could make my younger self inhale hard, hard enough to lodge that memory deep. To unearth in times of darkness.

We swept up the path to the peak, or so I thought. We stopped at a stone structure, which I took to be a guard tower or garrison of some sort, but then we were going up stairs for an interminable time. I could barely see anything, my younger self still with his eyes buried in my mother's side. We reached our destination, a warm room swaddled in rugs and furs, walls draped in ancient burgundy tapestries that had been punctured and woven with leafy vines that had snaked their way in from the window.

A bare-chested man sat there, his torso criss-crossed with scars that cut into a thick pelt of dark hair. Cern. Indigo cloth wrapped his hips and loins, held up with a frayed belt of braided animal hide. He leaned over, staring at a sleeping bundle of furs on the floor that I realized must have held a slumbering Maeve. My younger self went to him, bounded up the mountain of his lap to head butt him in the chest and gaze up at him. He wore a headdress of some sort, crested with bone, that hinted at a scalp scraped bald. The lines of hard laughter creased his face.

Cern's eyes looked back at my younger self, me, with an intensity that seemed odd towards a child, heavy with difficult love. "Sweet singer, my Baird. You are always welcome here, whether you come today or some tomorrow." His voice could have been rough-hewn velvet, grave but melodic. And he knew. *He knew I was there, side by side with my younger self. His next words were almost sub-vocalized, so that Fea and my mother wouldn't hear him. "If I seem hard, it is only because the things that will come weigh heavily on me. If I do not reach out for you, it is because you are a reminder of all that I've lost. Never think I or the black snake have anything but love for you."*

An iron thread of anger wove itself through the pain and love that my mother had inspired. He was not the only one who lost Anann of the Macha, Gentle Annie of the Black Bladed Death. And in his selfishness, he'd cost me a father where there had been no need.

The anger pulled me out of the hill's reverie. I awoke

with poison on my tongue and salt in my heart. The hill had given me a gift and a vendetta both. They did not settle easily in my chest. My senses came back to me slowly. I didn't notice at first that I was being held, strong arms putting me at a gentle angle. It could have been Fea, but it wasn't. Cern felt my body tense as I recognized him, and wisely began to extricate himself.

We were in the same room I'd just left, though the years had seen the wall tapestries completely eclipsed by the vines and ivy in from the window. Cern wore an open robe made of linen and fleece, a necklace strung with fine silver chains bearing gilded pinecones and silver-dipped twigs. He had aged, the hair on his chest now shot through with grey like a badger. Cern no longer wore the headdress, but fine stylized horns had been tattooed at his temples. His eyes had been drawn smoky with kohl.

Unsaid words bubbled up on his face, but they couldn't break the surface. Maybe he would have pushed them out, given them form, but I raised my palm and shook my head.

"Not now," I said. "Handle your dealings with Fea. Let me gather my wits." I paused. "Is it safe to travel the grounds?"

Fea squinted at me with suspicion. Cern turned his face from me reluctantly, and said to the floor, "Yes, of course. Walk about as much as you like."

Fea made her way next to the door as I left, gripped my hand and said, "We'll not be too brief, Baird. An hour or two at the least."

I nodded, took my hand back. "That's fine. I can occupy myself."

Fea nodded and let me go.

thliu's hidden keep was not vast, but the secrets in its walls whispered to me. They called my name. My fingers brushed along old stones that I swore must remember me as a youth. When my path took me near a swollen and puckered door, the whispers increased selfishly, begging me to pull on the knob. Behind it, an enclosed garden, swollen with shadows and sun. A massive oak sheltered a tipped over marble table and three small marble stools; a children's setting, likely toppled by the growth of the great tree.

The third chair gave me pause. Who had lived here besides myself and Maeve? I couldn't remember sitting there, but the stones knew where my eyes were drawn and they told me in broken tongues of how we'd laughed, how'd we'd played. How we'd planted an acorn there with naive encouragement. We'd told it to grow strong. The tree towered magnificently. Its branches were wide, heavy with leaves that brushed the tower window at its shoulder. I traced its branches with a finger, seized by both wonder and a sullen resentment of lost time.

I righted one of the little stools and sat with my spine against bark. This, then, was closer to my childhood eye level. But no real memories came to mind, not even a sliver of nostalgic sentiment to indicate that a tinier version of me had ever sat here. But the view showed more, though, than the walls had seen fit to explain in their hushed clamor. A pile of stones that we'd called a castle and played soldiers with. A scarred spot on the bark, scratch marks from a fox kit that we'd thought befriended but was likely rather terrified. A rough cube that had once been one of a pair of bone dice. Cern had carved the pips into with his knife, the stones told me.

I did not want to think of Cern. But when I rose to leave, one stone broke from its brethren to actually shout, *Not yet.* That was all it said, but still, I went to it, gingerly ran fingers over it. Tucked behind it lay an ancient slip of rolled paper, the state of it which truly made me feel my age, every century gliding off me with as if dew from a leaf.

I unwrapped it slowly, but even then, the edges left powdery smears on my fingers. It wasn't much, just a charcoal sketch of two faces. Another artist's hand trying to capture tuath form in two-dimensional form and failing. If I were honest, the hand was not unpleasant, and the artist had clear talent with lines and shadow. In judging its quality, I hadn't quite registered the two subjects. It could only be a portrait of Maeve and myself—but who had drawn it? And why was it hidden here? The stone in my hand somewhere conveyed an expectant silence. The day was still warm and yet I felt chills. I replaced it, pressing my palm against the stone of the wall, pushing with all of my birthright.

"Whose work is this?" I asked, filled with the Macha's gravitas.

The stones exhaled together with this name on their lips: *Brenna mac Ethliu.*

The name-sharing felt as if it should be more momentous. Like a bullet to my ribs. I wanted to sink to the floor in awed receipt of it.

But it meant nothing to me.

I texted Maeve: *Who is Brenna mac Ethliu?* But of course, here in Ethliu's court I had no signal, so the question lingered just the same as the memory. I left that garden, gold with sunlight and providence, as the stones kept up their susurrations. I fled the keep for the hillside. The grounds were quieter, the sun felt good on my face. But even here, the earth kept trying to impart wisdom and revelation.

A horrible realization bloomed in me. Maeve and I had always been told that we'd spent just a year on the hill with Cern, but these new memories were too rich and nuanced to be the events of a year. We were being lied to. Could Maeve know already? She sent me here. And she certainly had much more stature than I in our Court. Fea must know. And should have told me, of anyone.

I made a seat of the hillside, to put the keep in my view. It really was beautiful the way the stone began carved out of the rock, to then be bricked above into two towers. And a gatehouse, although I doubt that entrance still functioned. The centuries of ivy might be holding it together. This place, despite the secrets mortared into its walls, offered a comfort like home. The land did not ache with ill handling.

At some point I must have reclined, and at another I must have dozed. I woke and dozed and woke. I checked my phone again, but still no service. The grass felt like a hammock. One moment became the next. My eyes opened to an outstretched hand silhouetted against a blood orange sunset.

Fea pulled me to my feet, and we walked towards the keep, her arm draped comfortably around my shoulders. She wore a clean-smelling white tunic over jeans, her feet bare, and a smile carried easily enough for the both of us. My resentment had buried itself momentarily below my ribs, away from easy reach. Fea radiated joy just then, sun-kissed and light. Whatever the ritual she'd conducted with my father, it had left her in good shape.

She led me to a small room off the kitchen, probably once a servant's den, but appointed with mixed furnishings as if stolen from both a parlour and a country kitchen. The air carried the scent of rosemary and red wine. Cern hummed to himself, some notes treble and others basso profundo, accompanied by the measured cacophony of someone who knew their way around pots and pans. Fea pointed me towards a tufted leather armchair while she set the table and cut a fresh baked loaf into thick slices.

"Help with this, will you, Baird?" Cern asked, handing me an index card of terrible handwriting nearly a mirror of my own. Soon I was making a quick marinade and dicing onions, despite my misgivings.

This kitchen idyll wasn't foreign to me—Tadhg and I had dined like this for decades after first settling into my estate. But there with Cern and my mother's twin, the woman who'd raised me and then became my closest friend but was still not my mother, it felt like an incredibly pleasant betrayal. This was that familial warmth that I'd had to learn to create myself. The food made its way to the table, cabernet was poured. Cern asked for a brief incantation to Ethliu, and I managed not to flinch when he took my hand.

I stopped myself from ruining dinner by asking about Brenna mac Ethliu. I wanted to ask Maeve about it before I got myself into something more fraught than I was aware of. Fea and Cern talked about simple things. The vegetable gardens I hadn't yet seen. Some restorative work that Fea had been doing with her home. Beneath it all, the quiet warmth of Ethliu's saol. It surprised me a bit. Where was the sign of Ethliu's tragic decline? The worn-ness here served only to make things more comfortable and bore little resemblance to the dwindling fire I'd been told to expect.

I found myself staring at Cern, wondering what enchantment he'd wrought on me, that I would have forgotten entire years—decades?—of my life. Was he alone in doing so? Was Fea his accomplice even then?

Abruptly, I pushed my chair back from the table, a screech of wood on tile, and stood. Cern and Fea stopped talking, but I wouldn't explain myself.

"Fuck this," I muttered and just left. Fea might've called after me, I don't know. I needed to get off this damn hill.

I checked my phone again. It was just about half eight, so I'd be in the dark soon. But I didn't feel like going back and asking politely for a torch. On a lantern, even.

There was a moment, standing on an outcropping of shale, begging the sky for a tiny shred of phone signal so I could call Jimmy, where I could have sworn that I was being watched, but the feeling faded as I descended.

alfway down the hill, when I got signal again, I tried calling Kandace, but my service levels were still awful. I got a text through though: *C'mere K, be a dear and come fetch me from Athlone?*

Kandace: *no*

Me: *Please?*

Kandace: *i'll be there in an hour. you twat. i can't believe i'm going into the country for you.*

It would take twice that long for me to get off this tuathforsaken hill in the dark, but Kandace had a reputation for being late, so I decided not to tell her, instead texting her the pub's address: *Thanks, K. I'll meet you here.*

The dimming light silvered the evening and rendered everything in grayscale. I wondered if the hill would try to test me as I left but didn't really expect it to. The cut in the rock where I'd slipped into memory earlier let me pass without trouble.

The trouble came halfway down, when I saw a shadow

move the way it shouldn't. I couldn't presume it a trick of the light; there was a telltale queasy feeling in my gut. The shadow coagulated around a squirrel skittering on an overhead branch. The squirrel screamed as its spine and jaw warped, twisting out of shape and growing larger and more sinister. It leapt from the tree to the ground with a wet thud, eyes glassy and black, no longer screaming and instead eerily focused.

I looked about in the darkness but no ash tree casted down a prime branch for me fight it off, no stone sung out with prescient glee such that I might fling it into the creature's eyes—the hill's wood may not have it in for me, but it certainly wasn't offering any help. And I was no sage, head full of charms or words of power to ward off its attack.

So I ran. If the hill would not help me, I had no use for it.

The fell thing looked somewhat clumsy in its new skin. It took a moment to chase after me. Perhaps if it had been born from a stag instead of a squirrel I would have had less luck, but it's swollen paws were not so fleet on the forest floor.

I ran: wind in my eyes, bare feet bloodied by stones underfoot, branches slapping against my limbs like disdainful whips. And I could have lost it; the shore of Lough Derravaragh was not far, I could feel it. But at the base of the mount, I heard low sounds ahead of me, fevered grunting and the rhythmic slap of skin against skin. Was this a one-time tryst or a regular cruising spot? Either way, I couldn't draw this creature upon them.

I turned, sweat dripping into my eyes. The creature

stuttered to a brief stop, dark eyes glittered. It lunged at me, trying to knock me down. But the earth reached into me and leant me her strength—the impact bruised my side instead of knocking me down. I reached in close to its neck, hot breath rancid on my face. I scrabbled at bloody hanks of fur, skirting tendon to find windpipe; I pushed.

Its back legs frantically lashed out, scoring my side, but I could feel its fight dwindling, motions slowing. But when I expected to feel it die, the unnatural shadow abruptly let go of the squirrel's warped skin. The shadow skated along my arm, leaving frost in its wake, before drifting up into the trees, momentarily blotting out the starlight.

I stared at the sky, rubbing my arm and trying to place that sensation; it felt so familiar.

My phone vibrated in my pocket: *where you at? apparently no one in the pub has ever seen a black girl before. it's awkward.*

Half of my shirt in ribbons, no shoes, and I was bleeding from three places, including my lip somehow? And I had to figure out who to tell about this goddamn death squirrel.

I replied: *Around the corner. Order me a Guinness will you?*

Ah sure, I thought. It'll be grand.

aysus, Baird. Who tore you up?"

Now that we were safe in Kandace's battered Honda Civic, I had to answer her questions. I groaned and turned towards the window to press my face against the cool glass. Everything started to actually hurt now. My belly scratches throbbed.

"So you *can* die, but you won't die in my car? Just confirming."

I groaned. "Just take me home, please. To your home. I need to think."

"Fine, fine. But talk to me while you think."

"I got attacked…" I trailed off. There was sand all over the floor of the car. Maybe she'd been to the beach.

Kandace sighed. "No shit."

"I'm getting there, honest. It wasn't a normal thing. It was some kind of—" my hands flapped around while I thought of a word, "—a shadow … spirit? Of some sort?" Kandace let out a low whistle. "I don't know. It took over a squirrel, it got weird, it fucked me up. Then I killed it. But the spirit thing didn't die, it took off."

Rain began splattering the windshield in big wet drops. Kandace always left the wipers off until she absolutely needed them. It made me paranoid, but I didn't say anything for once. Her eyes were on the road. Her hands couldn't have been tighter on the wheel though.

"Why so quiet?" I asked. "You know something I don't?"

"No, no. Nothing like that," she said. "Spirit shit just freaks me out. How did you end up here anyway?"

I wanted to press her about that reaction, but when I'd done that before I had to put up with her ignoring my calls until she forgave me. Maybe whatever thing makes her more than human has something to do with "spirit shit." Which could be anything really.

"Baird? You in there? Why are we in fecking Athlone?"

My turn to sigh. I spilled the beans about Tadhg and Maeve, then about Fea and Cern. I didn't say anything about Brenna mac Ethliu. I still needed to sit down and scour my memory about her, see if there was anything else I could remember. I needed to call Maeve too.

The story got us nearly all the way to town. I felt a bodily sense of relief when Dublin enveloped me, not unlike the feeling of getting to my family's lands, but strictly psychological I suppose. Dublin was where I had the freedom to just be myself. No Court politics, no sulking consort, few obligations.

Kandace parked the Civic on the street outside her place, and as usual, didn't bother locking it. I mean, it was a piece of shite, true. Kandace claimed that leaving it unlocked meant that she never had to get the windows repaired when scumbags rifled through it. I rubbed my feet against each other as I got out, trying to get off as much of the blood-caked sand as I could.

Her flat was cluttered but clean, stacked with books and clothes and little objets d'art. I'd personally call them objets d'trash if she was out of earshot; our taste doesn't particularly overlap. Three drums, a guitar and a ukelele rested haphazardly beside the faded loveseat and the mandala-beaded pillows mounded on the floor.

Kandace made herself Earl Gray, me English Breakfast. Then she slipped away to the loo. When she came back, she wore a white vest, tracksuit bottoms and a hair bonnet. She dumped a bottle of antiseptic and some bandages next to my tea. After a second trip, she came back with an old shirt I must have left here a different night, gym shorts and a plastic SPAR bag.

I cocked an eyebrow at the pile.

"Do I have to?"

She just pointed at my bloody clothes. "Don't want you bleeding on all my shit."

"Fine, fine."

I laughed and started peeling everything off, wincing especially as I pulled my shirt out of the half-scabbed scratches. Kandace took everything, shoving it into the bag until it was bulging with my ruined wardrobe. Then she took to gleefully cleaning my wounds with antiseptic.

After I'd cleaned up and dressed, Kandace sat down across from me and took my hands, her expression serious. "Let me read you."

I hesitated. "I don't even know if I want to know."

"You do," she said. "Honest, you do."

I sighed, nodded a little.

A light bloomed between her closed eyes, a corona of sun caught in a swirling crescent. Fronds of orange gold that spun, unfurled and pulsed, like a kaleidoscope pointed at a copper nebula. The light retreated into her forehead like a flower closing its petals and she opened her eyes, face like she'd bitten a lemon.

"Someone's got their eye on you," Kandace said in a low

voice, heavy with new knowledge. "I didn't even have to go looking. They're right there, looming over you. Carrying the most casual malice I've ever seen. And a fierce hunger."

"What do they want?" I asked.

"I didn't get anything like that. As soon as they realized I was looking at them, the eye closed, and they were gone. I felt very *noticed* though. Didn't feel good."

"So now you're in danger," I said.

"Maybe," she admitted. "But I'm the one who demanded a reading."

"Fuck," I said. I looked around the room. Meanest looking object was a Ben Enwonwu coffee table book. "I should go."

Kandace snorted. "You think I can't keep my own place safe? Please, you insult me. They probably ran away because they were scared of me. Go to sleep and we'll tackle this in the morning." She stood up and stretched, yawning. "You wanna talk more or are you done for now?"

It was half twelve, and I could have done with a little more talking, but Kandace was clearly knackered.

"Nah, I'll probably potter about for a little while longer and then get some kip."

She nodded. "Want me to make the bed?"

"I know where everything is."

Her long fingers traced a wave, the pink beads she had in lieu of a proper door clacking against each other in her wake.

aybe Kandace could protect her flat from weird stuff, but her car was another story. The passenger side door had been ripped up, fabric torn to shreds, and the boot was wide open.

She knelt next to the seat, lying in the middle of the pavement, still in her night clothes. She inhaled deeply next to the carnage, wrinkling her nose. "Maybe it's your blood," she said, standing back up and going inside. I hunkered down to try and clean things up as best I could, but this wasn't really a problem that some quick tidying would solve.

When she came back, she held that SPAR bag full of my ruined clothes and wore a pair of dishwasher marigolds up to her elbows.

"What are you doing?"

Kandace didn't answer. She braided the rags together and then tied them into a bloody four-legged rag doll.

She pulled out a pen knife, circled me a few times looking at me like she didn't know where to begin. But eventually she stopped in front of me and gave up, just asked, "Baird, where is your ba?"

I frowned. "What's that?"

"Your aura maybe you'd call it? I need a slice of it."

"Hmm." I held out my arm. "I'm not sure I'd know where to look."

She held her hand about a foot away from my face, squinting at me. "It's usually about here. Emanates from your body."

"It emanates from...oh!" I laughed. "I think I know what you mean. Well, I can't see them, but even if I could, you can't see your own right? And why's that?"

"Are you quizzing me? Because you're inside it. Can't see the forest for the trees."

I nodded. "You are having the same problem."

Kandace's eyes narrowed. "Stay still." She stalked down the pavement in her bare feet, often stopping to turn around and squint back at me. Eventually, she stopped, shrugged and walked back to me.

"Fuck," she said.

"I am tuath," I said.

"No," she said. "I mean, that's cool or whatever but I don't know how to shave a wee bit off the edge because your ba is so big."

"Does it hurt?" I asked.

"Yup." She made a quick little slice, and it did.

Pain blistered my skull, made me blind for a moment, and must have knocked me to my knees, because when I came to I was face to face with the strangest cat I'd ever seen. A hairless Egyptian sphinx, eyes filled with a light that could only be my own. Its veins gleamed blue under that wrinkled, pale skin.

Kandace made a sweeping gesture. The cat yowled in recognition, and then it tore off.

"Think of her as a spiritual decoy," she said. "Now, let's go buy some duct tape. You got a plan for after we clean up this mess?"

I nodded. "I'm in the mood for petit fours, aren't you?"

I woke at about dawn to a shriek, and then a shatter. Nora had dropped her mug on the ground. "Baird? What are you doing here?"

I put my head back down on the velvet pillow. "Your mistress will be here in about an hour. She'll expect breakfast." I pointed at Kandace, sleeping on the couch. "This is Kandace. She'll probably want a few croissants. Do you have any protections on the door?" Nora's entry hall was several rooms away, through a foyer bedecked with at least five ancient mirrors, one marble bust and more terrible stoic portraits than I cared to count. Any of those could be otherworldly in nature.

"Protections?" she echoed. "There's just Jenny...where *is* Jenny?"

I frowned, pointing behind me at her greathound, a puddle of fur that took up rather more room on the massive couch than I did. "That must be my friend here. Maeve told me you were marked."

Nora's hand flitted nervously to a place between her breasts and her cheeks flushed pink.

"Did she not tell *you*?"

"Of course she told me—" Nora started.

"Put the kettle on," I interrupted, too weary to be polite. "She'll have to tell you when she gets here."

Kandace yawned and sat up then, blinking wearily at Nora. "Oh, hello." A slight predatory note in Kandace's greeting made me look at Nora with fresh eyes, finally noting the shimmery chemise that dipped below her dressing gown, her sheepskin slippers, and the faint remains of last night's makeup. Not an item on her that hadn't been bought in Brown Thomas, most likely, but yes, in this light, she did have the vulnerable doe-quality that Kandace usually went for.

Jenny uncurled herself from behind me and walloped herself around, all nine or ten stone of her. The frames shook on the walls until she settled down again after thoroughly licking everyone's face.

I introduced them and went to the jacks. When I returned, the kettle was on the boil and Kandace smoked out the window while Nora looked enchantingly scandalized. I passed the time watching Kandace make her own mark—which she did somehow while talking about construction and the collapse of the Celtic Tiger—until Maeve's car pulled up the drive, a sleek black BMV. It had started raining at some point. St. Claire got out of the car with an umbrella to open the backseat, resplendent in tight blue jeans and a waistcoat atop a crisp white shirt. However, my heart dropped when, instead of Maeve, my consort unfolded himself from the car and stepped out.

Tadhg took the umbrella and peered up at the windows while St. Clair fetched his bag from the boot, a single dark leather duffel. Tadhg had worn his hair down today, swept back over his shoulder in a waist-length fall of gold.

I turned away from him to the two in the sitting room. "I hate to interrupt this delightful conversation, but we have a visitor."

Nora made a pleased sound, no doubt still expecting Maeve. Perhaps Kandace had not been as successful as she'd hoped in intriguing Nora. Or, even if she had, it couldn't compare to the anticipation of a tuath's attention. But then, she *had* succeeded in distracting Nora long enough that she was still in her nightclothes. So, perhaps it was still a win. I met Kandace's eyes and made a mew of disappointment towards the window.

The doorbell rang. Nora hurried to the door.

"I can't pretend to interpret that. Use your words." Kandace threw her cigarette butt onto the stone path below and closing the window.

I pointed to the sound. "Not Maeve. Tadhg."

Kandace kissed her teeth. "Your—"

"Yes."

"Oh hello, I expected—"

Tadhg swept into the room like a jagged gust of wind, all floppy wool coat and scarf for miles, everything unwinding as he settled on the couch beside me, all without the slightest contact. He patted Jenny's big grey head absent-mindedly. She knew not to trifle with him the way she had with me, jumping about and putting her paws everywhere. Tadhg stared at Kandace with increasing confusion, his face twisting from side to side like a finch. A slow smile spread across

Kandace's face until she seemed on the verge of cackling.

Just shy of Kandace's hysteria, Tadgh extended his hand gravely. "Tadgh mac Muir."

"Howarya. Kandace O'Flaherty."

Tadhg's head did a bird twitch again at her accent and Kandace couldn't help it, she chortled. "What is she?" he asked me in Irish.

"Not tuath," she said, in Irish as well. "They teach it in school now, you know. Also, none of your business. Next you'll be asking me where I'm *from*." She gestured with scare quotes. Pain spasmed on Tadhg's face at the faux pas, but Kandace switched back to English and kept talking without a bother. "Delighted to make your acquaintance, however. I've heard a lot about you from your man. I didn't know you'd be—"

"Such a harridan?" he asked.

"—so tall!" Kandace finished.

"Yes, well, Baird's ego dwarfs even me." He met my eye, but I certainly wouldn't challenge him. "Your text sent Maeve into a...well. A tizzy is slightly too strong a word."

"A tizzy," Kandace echoed.

Tadhg shot her a sharp glance and Kandace looked appropriately cowed. "Where did you hear that name, Baird?"

I crossed my arms over my chest, only now feeling like maybe I should have girded myself better. Gym shorts and a vest were hardly the armor best worn for a fight with Tadhg anywhere but a bedroom. "From the grounds of Cern mac

Ethliu."

"From the grounds?" Tadhg repeated.

I shrugged. "There was a drawing. When I asked the keep who drew it, the name came to me."

His eyebrow cocked up. I noticed that he woreg the thinnest sliver of coral on his brow—the crown he'd worn when I met him, and he was just the youngest prince of the Muir, my Court's deadliest enemies. It made me nervous. One of the reasons we'd come together had been my poor aptitude for ritual or power; as tuath went, the Muir had little time for mystery. The sea was mysterious enough for them. But that crown. It gave the scions of the Muir the strength of the sea, even when they were far from shore.

"I know," I said. "But I couldn't have mistaken it for anything else. What did Maeve say? Why did she send you instead of coming herself?"

"Fea asked her to stay. She said that she needed Maeve and Granddame to be there."

"Perhaps to see if she was with child."

"What?" Tadgh asked. "How?"

I grimaced. "I may have another sibling soon. Fea met with Cern too."

Tadhg looked accusingly at Kandace as if he had been the only one to not know. She held up her hands for mercy. "I'm just hearing this part now. Tuath business is not my business. I'll check on breakfast."

"Kandace—" I started, just her name.

"Don't worry, just to supervise. You know I've never met

a pan I can't burn or a toaster I can't ruin."

We both laughed. Jenny followed at her heels, perhaps looking forward to an errant dollop of butter.

"What is she?" Tadhg asked again when Kandace had left. "And please tell her I didn't mean to come across as a racist wanker. Is it safe for her to go into the kitchen or does she have to touch the microwave to ruin it?"

"Oh—" I laughed again. "No. Kandace is just a terrible cook. And despite that being a rude question, I think? I don't know *what* she is, just who she is. And that's a friend."

I wasn't sure if Tadhg would pursue the line of questioning or not, but he left it alone. He picked up his duffel and set it in his lap to rummage within. Eventually he withdrew a wine dark bag with a neck that had been sealed with wax. He dropped it in my lap before taking Kandace's seat opposite me. "She told me to give you this. Open it please, I'm dying to know what it is."

The bag had some slight heft, but the seal was the heaviest part of it. I cracked the seal and upended it, to find that the bag had contained a necklace of three hammered pieces of brass on a sinewy thong. A single disc flanked by two crescent moons. The full moon had been marked with the glyph for passion: Maeve. The waning moon for song: Baird. And the waxing moon for the raven: Bran. Or, if the raven was feminine: Brenna.

I have walked Eire for hundreds of years, even if time passes differently for tuath than it does for men. Always, I have walked it beside Maeve, or in her shadow. The idea that there might have been a third with us was—well, unfathomable. It split me open.

I didn't notice when Tadhg got up and sat beside me again, or when he examined the necklace. Only when Kandace pressed a steaming cup of tea into my hands, and Tadhg laced his fingers beneath mine to ensure that I wouldn't drop it, did I realized he was holding me. I'd been keening, a lost sound. My cheeks flushed, to think I'd been brought so low by grief for someone I'd never known. Or had I? That drawing...I didn't understand. And Maeve had known?

"What did she say when she gave it to you?" I asked Tadhg, brittle in his arms. I didn't deserve his kindness but I didn't want him to stop.

"Nothing. She just said to go to you." His voice was so deep for such a lanky vessel; it rumbled through me like a drum.

"May I?" Kandace asked Tadhg, her palm extended. Tadhg placed the necklace in her hand at my nod.

The lightshow that erupted from her head surprised a murmur from Tadhg, but he simply watched as her corona swelled and pulsed at her brow. When it retracted back into her inner eye, Kandace opened her eyes thoughtfully. "The hungry goddess watches, still. I can't get much."

"You didn't give them a gender before," I observed. "But now...?"

Kandace shrugged. "It seemed apt. And the presence is *big*. Even bigger than your mythical arses."

"We have few gods, barring ourselves," I said. The Three-in-One were the only 'goddess' that the Macha paid fealty to. The Muir only begged succor from the sea.

"The hungry goddess…" Tadhg echoed. "Ethliu?"

"But you saw something," I suggested. "Something she let you see."

"This necklace has spent much time with Maeve. It has been perfumed in her ba, more than any other. I'd say the watcher finds Maeve's power tantalizing, but too dangerous. Which makes me think that, well—"

"Baird might be the perfect snack," Tadhg said, mouth sour. He looked skyward and then back at me. "You mentioned earlier that Fea had gone to him to try and conceive. Why did she think it would work, considering the state of the saol?"

I looked sharply at Tadhg. "Do you know something I don't?"

He equivocated with a wave of his arm. "I'm not above eavesdropping on phone calls. I heard Ciara asking Granddame about it. So I reached out to my fathers."

I blinked. He hadn't spoken to his fathers since his mother had gone into the sea, what, a century ago? Despite her absence, his fathers still ruled Court of the Muir, Tadhg's elder sister carrying out all ceremonial functions like meeting with the merrow people. "After all this time…"

"I know," he said, acknowledging my expression. "But it felt important. And it's true of the Muir as well. No one has been born to us in a ré."

Worry worked its way up my back. Tadhg was younger than me, in the grand scheme of things, but what was time to the tuath? I could remember a hunt that took me through a wood for the course of an afternoon, begging swiftness from my steed and ducking under vexing tree branches as we rode, only to find when I returned without a stag but having drank from a pool hidden in the heart of a virgin glade, my head swimming with new and heavy mysteries, that while I had been gone, an entire war between the Riven and the Muir had felled half my family, the saol surging into me upon my return. Time could only be inconsequential and fickle.

Still, this problem was grave. And I resented having it dropped on me, when I'd rather deal with the question literally in my lap. "Why haven't Maeve, Fea and Granddame dealt with this already?" I tried not to whine but know that I failed.

"Maybe if you—" Tadhg started but Kandace held up a hand. The bejeweled snake necklace around her neck writhed.

Nora chose an inopportune moment to return with a tray laden with toast and tea. She'd changed, and now wore a lovely knee-length blue frock with full sleeves, her hair pinned up like a 1950s American housewife, all framed beautifully by the light coming in through the shimmery grey curtains at the bay window. Which was abruptly blotted out by darkness.

I tackled her as the window shattered, glass raining down everywhere amidst a snarling cyclone of black shadow and teeth. The more I looked at it, shielding Nora's heaving body with my own, the more its features clarified. Four legs, a vicious snout with teeth that shivered in the light, bristling fur. Another shadow like the one on Cern's hill. Poor Jenny. The shadow had taken her.

The beast lunged for Kandace, but her necklace had slithered from her neck and now Kandace swung it like a whip, citrine and topaz flashing. It hesitated long enough for her to jump up onto the sectional. Another threatening lash caught it on the nose, kept the thing at bay.

My consort beckoned one of Nora's mirrors to flow quicksilver-like from the wall, the glistening shape of it becoming a spear, sharp as Tadhg's own reflection.

"Get up, Baird," Tadhg said stepping in front of me

He didn't have to ask me twice. I heaved off of Nora, getting her to her feet and pushing her gently to the door.

"Lock yourself in a room," I tried to tell her.

But she wouldn't go.

Tadhg's spear point thrust unerring towards the creature, catching it in its belly before it twisted away. The noise it made seemed awfully familiar.

"Jenny?" Nora asked, disbelieving.

The creature showed no sign of recognizing her, only whining in frustration that it couldn't feed. Its head looked cannily around the room. Too late, I realized it intended to escape. I bent down to get the tray, thinking I might be able to fend it off with something in my hands, but I moved too slow. Just as Tadhg thrusted his spear at it again, the dark beast leaped over me to freedom.

We panted and recovered. Kandace had the wherewithal to comfort Nora, who stared at the spilled crockery like it was unmanageable. Poor thing was in shock.

Tadhg pivoted between me and Kandace. "Why are you both so unperturbed by this? What else haven't you told me? What else is going to—"

"For feck's sake, Tadhg, stop. There's a reason no one tells you things and it's because you're like a dog with a bone about it."

At the mention of the word 'dog,' Nora broke down and started sobbing. Kandace huffed at me and took her out of the room.

I told Tadhg about the squirrel on Cern's hill, and the subsequent mauling of Kandace's car. His expressions made the telling of it all feel much more dire than I'd acted about it earlier. Perhaps because I had less reason to act cavalier about my problems around Tadhg. He'd mopped up so many of mine before.

At the end of the story, Tadhg groaned and got to his feet, gathering up his long coat from where it had fallen behind a settee and winding his scarf back around his neck. "You are honestly such a child, Baird. You've been hunted by this thing for two days and you haven't bothered looking into it?"

Half-uttered sounds of protest made their way out of my mouth. "I was obviously going to. After I talked with Maeve."

"No," Tadhg said wearily. "You were going to make

Maeve deal with it. Which is not the same thing. Come, let's call a car. We need to make a social visit. Do you have anything nicer than that to wear?"

"Just a t-shirt but it will have to do. Kandace can probably drive us, let me ask—hold on a second." I interrupted myself as Tadgh withdrew a pair of charcoal slacks and a cream polo shirt from his duffel bag. "You travelled with clothes for *me?*"

Tadhg blew an errant lock of gold from his face. "I didn't want to have to be seen anywhere with you looking unpresentable."

I could feel my blood pressure rising, along with my volume. "Where are we going that it matters even the tiniest what I look like?"

Tadhg plucked his phone from his pocket and pulled up a location. I clocked the D4 address and sighed. "You're right," I said. The vest had tea all over it anyway. With Nora out of sight, I shucked everything off, shivering a little from the open window., I held out my hands for the change of clothes. But Tadhg didn't budge. "I said you were right. What else do I need to say? C'mon, Tadhg."

Tadgh put the clothes down behind him. The end table was covered with shards of glass and smeared butter. He swept it off with one motion and undid the buckle on his trousers.

"Tadhg," I said weakly. I covered my knob, not because I was modest—I'd no reason for that, nor shy temperament— but because I didn't want him to see the reaction he was getting.

He shook his head slowly and undid his fly. His eyes sparked like flint under his brows.

I wasn't going to beg him to stop. I didn't want to. Without being asked, I bent over the hardness of the table, my hands flat on the cold wood. Tadhg's buckle clattered against the pin as his trousers fell to his knees.

He talked dirty in the old language while he fucked me, calling me names over and over again: Lover. Fool. Heartbreaker. When I tried to reply, to say anything, he shoved long fingers into my mouth, so I sucked on them instead. He came with a thundering cry and collapsed against my back, still fully clothed. He laid there for some time, breath hot on my neck. my own need throbbed, untended to and crushed against the side of the table.

Kandace's heavy footsteps trod above us, getting close to the stairs. "Tadhg," I said. An entreaty.

He levered himself off me, trousers up and zipped before I even regained control of my limbs. The hair on my chest was matted with blood, cut by a half dozen fragments of glass that Tadhg had missed. I whistled appreciativelyg, but Tadhg wouldn't look at me.

"Get dressed," he said.

I hadn't realized I wanted it to be a reconciliation fuck until it became clear it was nothing of the sort.

I kept my back straight. I collected the fresh clothes he'd brought me and walked past him to the bathroom. I'd thought to finish myself off, since he hadn't done me the courtesy, but somewhere between him and the bathroom I found myself weeping. Not like Nora earlier, but still. So instead I ran a quick shower and cleaned myself up.

I emerged cleaned up, somewhat calm, and carrying a bundle of bloody towels. Certainly didn't want to lure Jenny back here to Nora again.

Kandace and Tadhg were drinking fresh cups of tea and there was no sign of Nora, or of the mess the creature had made, if I ignored the empty window. "Nora is calling someone to come board it up," Kandace explained. "She has to get the glass special ordered from London and it might take a week."

Tadhg put down his mug. "Let's go."

We crunched down the gravel drive to Kandace's car. She looked at Tadhg with an apology when she popped the boot. There was barely any room. He waved her off. I sat in the back without being told. One glance at the sandy floor had him turn at Kandace. "You surf?"

She looked back at him with appreciation. "Yeah, I was at Perfect Wave the day I got dragged into this mess."

"Deadly," he said. "Nothing like it. If I weren't tuath, I'd swear god was a wave at Mullaghmore."

Kandace's eyes lit up. "Have you been to Aill na Searrach yet?"

"Bless her wave, sweet Aileen," Tadhg said, giving a chef's kiss to his fingers.

I should have known this would happen. I groaned and sunk down, making a pillow out of whatever I found on the back seat. Might as well get some kip while they nerded out.

 woke to Kandace shaking my leg. She ate chips out of an Abrakebabra bag. "I can't go in, but you have to, Tadhg says."

"What?" I rubbed my eyes.

"Only tuath allowed," she said. "Chip before you go in?"

I shoved a few into my mouth and got up. Tadhg waited, silhouetted in front of a floodlight. With...two others? In front of a stone tower. I could hear the sea, but this wasn't the Gaita estate. Where were we?

"Baird mac Macha, well met." A throaty contralto with a BBC accent. Not Og, then. And Thahliah hadn't been seen since—

"Caoimhe!" I said warmly. I bounded forward a bit and embraced her. She'd had her hand held out for shaking, or kissing perhaps, so she didn't expect it. "I haven't seen you in far too long."

Caoimhe poked me in the chest. I stopped myself from wincing by slathering on a grin. She was a vision of serenity and freckled cream, dark red hair pulled back in a severe knot that made her features look carved from marble. "That's because my father told you that he didn't want to see you for at least a decade after you showed up drunk in the middle of that ceremony."

I waved that off, along with a strange ghost of feeling. I

didn't recognize it right away; I'd almost forgotten that the Gaita were the only Court whose glamour worked on other tuath. A poor lesson to forget, considering her father Og was the first tuath I'd ever trysted with. "No, still. That was at least forty years ago."

"Perhaps," Caoimhe said doubtfully. "This is my love, Niamh. They're of the Boirinn."

"Oh," I said, registering the pronoun, peering through the light. "I've heard of you." I held out my hand to clasp arms.

"Have we met?" Shaved head, jacked arms, no-fucks-given expression. Smoking hot. If I were butter, I'd have melted. Their hand rested on the back of a white furred creature, even bigger than Jenny, but resembling e a cross between a hare and a goat. When it looked up at me, and big golden eyes staring out of its head, I realized it was a púca.

"No," I said. "but I heard a story—"

"Don't mind him, Niamh. He has poor impulse control," Tadhg said cruelly. "It's an ongoing struggle."

Caoimhe glanced up at the moon. Just a sliver of it in the sky, barely visible amongst the clouds. I checked my phone. It was 9:30pm. "We should head in. The library is not organized like you might expect."

Caoimhe led us along a path of carefully cut interlocking pavement stones. The path meandered amidst low-lying shrubs and statuary, the air thick with the perfume of night-blooming jasmine. Instead of heading into the tower, as I expected, she brought us down a flight of carved stone towards the cliff face. "If you'd come to me two days from now, we would not have been able to help you," Caoimhe said. I didn't understand her, until I saw her draw on the moonlight to beckon the door. The cliff did not *want* to be a door, but it would, only for the moon. By door of course, I mean a yawning opening in the stone. The cavern exposed by the door held a honeycomb of caverns, each lit by a tightly sconced flame that burned without fuel.

I looked at Niamh, who took up the rear along with the púca. "Your people's work, I assume?"

They nodded absent-mindedly, opening and closing their fist, a spark of the Boirinn's ever-burning fire sparking between their fingers. "Hurry," they said. "It won't hold for long unless it's a clear night."

It was disconcerting, to say the least, stepping through a space that might become solid rock if an errant cloud were to get in the way of the moon. I followed Tadhg inside and refused to look back. I don't think I was claustrophobic, per se, but I didn't need to test that right now. The shelves of the Gaita's library had been carved into the stone within dozens of niches, some of which were large enough for a desk and two chairs, others only wide enough for a tuath to turn around in. They weren't organized by author, Caoimhe explained. They were organized by era, and by subject. The oldest records were in fact a collection of objects inscribed with runes, glyphs and sigils, harkening back before the 11th century, before paper became more common.

"Tadhg told us a little bit about the creature," Caoimhe

said. "But tell us again about the first time you met it."

I explained again about the squirrel creature, but it seemed like I presented little new from Tadhg's explanation. She shuffled me off to a gloomy alcove filled with texts devoted to Court manifestations, while she and Tadhg went elsewhere.

I noted that, instead of heading into the stacks, Niamh sat down at a table near me and set a Boirinn flame to the empty sconce there. They fed it somehow until the light became incandescent. It brightened up my corner considerably. "Cheers," I said. "Not up for helping us look?"

They shook their head. "I'm nearly blind. That's why I drag poor Kells here around with me." They gave the púca at their feet an affectionate scratch behind the ears. It flickered in shape while they scratched, appearing briefly as an all-white dog, then a bear, then a massive badger, before returning to its original in-between shape.

I sucked my teeth. "Sorry," I said. "I hadn't noticed."

"No worries. But if you find something that seems promising, I have my magnifier and can help. Most of these texts don't have ebook versions unfortunately."

I snickered and went back to my shelf. "True. I'll let you know if I find anything."

The array of volumes was fascinating, even to someone as un-academically minded as myself. Many were handwritten, journals really. And less from the Court of the Gaita than I expected. Where had they come across this scrap from the journal of Ern, an ancient matriarch of the Macha? It might have been the oldest description of the Triple Aspect that I'd ever seen, coming after she'd brought her daughter into the world. Only later, when I read that the daughter's name was Badb, did I realize she was talking about Granddame .

After Tadhg's eventual crow of excitement was lucky, we met at Niamh's table. Tadhg lay down a tome thick with dust and a massive femur, which raised my eyebrow until I recognized the carvings that covered its length. Niamh took the bone and examined the marks with their magnifying glass, exhaling sharply about halfway down.

"This was a sacrifice to end winter," they said. They read further and went pale, nearly dropping the bone, but stopping themselves and instead placing it down carefully. "A tuath sacrifice."

"Yes." Tadhg nodded "Or close enough not to matter. According to this—" he said, patting the book and earning another cloud of dust, "—it likely belong to Elatha." Caoimhe made a sound deep in her throat. Niamh looked like they wanted to wash their hands. "This complicates things."

Caoimhe nodded.

"How?" Niamh asked.

I cleared my throat. "I still don't know who—"

Caoimhe touched my elbow to stop me. I ignored the thrill her glamour sent up my spine. "Bree's father. Of the Riven."

"Who apparently," Tadhg continued, "was used to wake Ethliu by an Accord of the Courts."

"To *wake* her?" Niamh sounded skeptical.

Tadhg cleared his throat to read some verse. It didn't rhyme in English: "*When the black snake coils in the earth's bones, unwilling to cede the land to bud, beckon her. In fire and blood, she rises, of full breast and grizzled beard. In the lightning's wake, bark cracked and glistening with sap, she conjures new growth. Give her your ill-cast children, your undreamed future heirs. She will grind them to ash and seed the new dawn.*"

"Gruesome," I pronounced it.

Caoimhe shrugged. "Perhaps she is from before the tuath. An old one. We could study the truly ancient archives…" she trailed off as she pointed to the wall laden with hundreds of pottery fragments and jewelry, an endless undertaking.

"The Court of the Ethliu was small, but powerful," Tadgh read out loud. "And made up of tuath from four influential Courts: the Riven, the Muir, the Boirinn and the Macha."

"I've never heard this before," Niamh confessed. "Tadhg, did you——"

"No. Never."

Niamh winced. "The Boirinn were always… well, *cruel* when they talked about your father, Baird."

"But why——" Understanding dawned in me. "Oh. That's why no one is joining the Ethliu. They wanted their complicity to die with the Court."

"The Accord ended some centuries ago, when the Riven fell out of disfavor," Tadhg continued.

I snorted. "This must have been written by a Muir." The

Muir *massacred* the Riven. That was the deed that brought the Macha and the Muir to war, until Tadhg and I were joined.

Tadhg glared at me until Caoimhe made him continue. "And they haven't fed anyone to Ethliu since then." Tadhg turned a few pages and pointed at a rough illustration. "Which brings us to the Hunger."

We all peered at the drawing. The sketch resembled a fox been hammered flat and stretched, emaciated and thin. Then blackened and littered with jagged teeth, wicked bone spurs that protruded from its back and haunches. I only had to look for a moment to know that this was the creature that had hunted me. That had taken over Nora's hound.

It was good to have a name for it. The Hunger.

"So what has she been eating?" Niamh asked.

"It's tried to eat me twice now," I said. "No, three times."

"Not the Hunger." Niamh shook their head. "The goddess. Ethliu."

I had no idea. Caoimhe looked nervously at her stacks, has if she might throw herself into further research just to stop herself from fretting about it. I nearly jumped when Tadhg slammed the book shut in disgust.

"Oh, come now," he said, punctuating his talk with punches to the tome. "We *know* what she's been eating. Who was born during the Age of Battles? All four of us, and the other handful that make up our generation. How many have been born since then? No one. What did the Age follow? Ethliu's unwilling fast."

"Please, Tadhg. The book." I slid it away from my consort

towards Caoimhe who picked it up carefully and clutched it to herself.

Tadhg kept going as if nothing had happened. "Your bloody *saols*, you fools. From all our Courts. I bet the future of the Muir that Ethliu has been taking the saols of our dead as long as we've been alive."

Into the shocked silence that followed, my mind became a blank slate. I had to tell Maeve. I looked at my phone; four bars, thank feck. *Call me*, I texted her. Then I noticed the three missed calls. And the text from Kandace that just said *OUTSIDE*.

"For feck's sake," I said and jumped to my feet so quickly that the púca growled at me. "I have to get out. Caoimhe let me out of here."

Caoimhe trailed me back to where we'd entered, her diaphanous skirts trailing behind her. "I might not be able to open it right away," she said.

"Yes, you will," I replied. "You have to."

But despite her fears, she summoned door in the stone was easily and I threw myself through it. The paving stones flew by as I raced back to the car. The cloud of beaks and feathers that buffeted Kandace's car made me gasp.

"Oi, get off her," I shouted, well before considering what I would actually do when I caught their attention, and the black shapes became a heaving mass of cacophonous sound and beak. They'd one been seagulls, I guessed.

Tadhg stood beside me, a new spear with him, and I wondered what ancient mirror of the Gaita had been lost so that Tadhg didn't have to keep a smaller, more portable weapon. He grunted and I took the war hammer he proffered me, a heavy spiked thing that didn't look so different from the awful birds in the sky.

Kandace threw herself out of the back seat as soon as there was room, that strange necklace of hers slithering into her hand.

"What were you—"

She unfurled her jewelled whip. "I thought I'd get some kip in the backseat."

Tadhg looked at Kandace's weapon in askance until she dropped the first black bird from the sky with a crystalline crack. Two more seagulls joined the first, while Tadgh thrust at them in vain. The birds were hard to see against the darkness of the sky.

"I can't see much at all," Niamh muttered beside me. "Are they getting them?"

"Kandace is," I said quietly.

Between assaults, Niamh touched Kandace's elbow, and after a moment's conferment, Niamh woke an undying flame on her whip. Now, when Kandace attacked, the fire flashed against the sky and we knew that the Hunger could not tolerate Niamh's flame. One gull's wings got afire and flew into the flock. The night filled with awful cries and smoke and burning feathers.

I was useless, but hardly minded. "Where's Caoimhe?" I asked Niamh, who gestured back towards the library.

"She thought of something," Niamh said. "Another text

she had to read. She wouldn't leave it."

I shrugged. "She'd be even less help than me in a fight, wouldn't she?"

"Aye, unless it was at a dinner table."

I mock shuddered. "I don't need any help starting fights at dinner."

A cry of triumph split the air; Tadgh had figured out how to spin his spear like a baton; he shred an attacking seagull as if it had passed through a particularly violent industrial fan. Kandace laughed with him and I rolled my eyes strictly for my own benefit. They'd won some reprieve, I think, the Hunger abandoning the birds like it had the squirrel, and, I suspected, Jenny, leaving them behind like bruised husks while it spirited itself away.

A third cry joined then, but from the Library's direction, and for a moment I worried that it might have been one of pain. But instead it was Caoimhe, lit from behind by a stray waft of moonshine, running towards us, a sheaf of old papers in her arms. Her beauty caught me in its net until I shook it off.

"Look," she said, and began rolling out the sheafs on Kells's broad back as if it were a table. The púca snorted with a long-suffering expression until it was hard to see beneath the papers. Caoimhe pointed at two places in the pages, cramped writing surrounded by tiny illustrations, impossible to pick out until Niamh summoned their fire. Writing that looked oddly familiar.

"Look," Caoimhe said again. "What does it say?"

"This one says, hmm. Let's see." I squinted. The writing might look familiar, but the dialect was unpracticed. "This is an old tongue."

Tadhg ducked in under my arm to read it. "This is about Springtime. Ending the dark of Winter. Feeding the tree. Very dramatic. To wake the sleeping dragon in the bones of the earth, then if…wait, who wrote this?"

I knew where I recognized the handwriting. "Cern," Caoimhe and I said at the same time, but where she said it with excitement at having solved a riddle, I said it with distress. The recipe card.

"You didn't read far enough," she said. "There are diary notes. Accords of his own that Cern made. With each of your Courts."

Tadhg, Niamh and I exchanged hesitant looks.

"Accords for…" Niamh couldn't bring themselves to say it.

Tadhg exhaled sharply. I think he knew.

"An unborn tuath with every ré," Caoimhe said, from rote. And I knew she'd read the notes often enough that she was sure, so I didn't bother asking. Instead, I thought only of a name: *Brenna*. Dear lost sister.

"What have they done?" Tadhg asked, but no one answered.

"And the saol…" Niamh said, unwilling to look away from what Caoimhe had uncovered.

Caoimhe cleared her throat. "That part is clear: *The Courts may think that they can abandon my lady whaen she is no longer convenient for them. But their binding runs deeper than words, and I will seek her will done here in Eire.*"

I closed my eyes. The words were easier to say to the backs of my eyelids. "So he knows exactly what he's doing. There's no way I can save him, even if I wanted to."

"Baird, he's your father, but this—"

"No, I understand," I said, gripping Tadhg's hand until I realized I had no business doing so. Kandace squeezed my shoulder. "What are these other pages?" I asked, pointing to the stack Caoimhe kept in her arms. "Prophecies, visions, portents. Drawings of same." She rifled through them. "Nothing that—oh. Well. There's this, actually. I didn't make the connection before." She withdrew a whispering page from the sheaf, its age apparent, and flipped it towards us. More chicken scratch, yes, but also a face. With three horizontal lines across each cheek.

We all turned slowly towards Kandace, whose fingers had risen up of their own volition to touch her face. "But this must be decades old. I'm only twenty-four."

Our gaze didn't waver. My eyebrow shot up. Kandace had never told me much of her nature. I regretted that now.

"In this body," Kandace snapped, self-consciously returning her whip to its place, trying not to squirm as the whip settled around her neck like a dog finding its favorite place on the couch. "It's mostly true. But I have dreams of another time. I have … memories of things. Not of this though, I promise."

I frowned in thought, wondering what might be in

Kandace's head.

"No, honest," shae said, interpreting my face correctly, screwing up her face as she tapped into those memories. "The things I remember aren't of Ireland. They're of the steppe, and of huge armies, moving in formation. I—well, I think I was a general. Or a ruler. In a past life."

"Pity you weren't an assassin," Tadhg said, but it was a small joke, for him anyway.

"What does the prophecy or whatever say?" Niamh asked, ever on topic. Caoimhe shook her head. "Nothing concrete. It's pictorial. General sense of doom from her arrival, I think. There are some notes written on the scroll next to it."

We leaned in to read, but it seemed inconsequential. Halfway through reading, while Kandace waited for us, unable to read ancient tuath script, she gasped. "What is that?" she asked, pointing to an odd grid of faces, where yes, her face again was repeated in an alternating row of boxes, juxtaposed with repetitive geometry in shaded pencil.

"The text beneath it..." Tadhg murmured. "It says: *Ethliu's hunger cannot die, only slumber, lest a queen's tongue demand her death. But her thirsts fill my dreams, make me ache in the daylight with their memory. Begging for blood, for salt. Thrice denied, once reclaimed. She would swallow the land, and still be hungry. I take cold comfort that the sea is too great for her to drink.*"

Kandace's arms crossed her chest and a sound like a squeak left her lips.

"What? No judgement, friend. We all know so little."

"Will you promise not to laugh?" Her voice was unusually small.

"On the Macha," a said.,

My friend exhaled sharply. "I wasn't born Kandace. I took that name for myself. In the memories… I thought they were dreams. And the armies. They called me Kandace when they addressed me. It wasn't really my name then, either."

"I don't understand, love," Niamh said, voice gentle.

"I think it was my title," Kandace explained. She ground her boot into the pavement beneath us. "It means—I think it means Queen."

"Lest a Kandace's tongue…" Caoimhe said, wondering.

"And the drawing." Kandace sounded more and more like her old self, now that her revealed secret wasn't met with scorn. "I've drawn that before. My old self has. On leather, I think. A long strip of leather…it's a spell. A warding spell."

I stared at the drawing. I was so far out of my depth. I looked between Tadgh and Niamh. "Cern must be confronted, and soon. By the Courts that caused this mess. Those still standing, anyhow." There was no accounting for the lost Court of the Riven. "But I worry that there is more that we are missing, that might be uncovered."

"Are you asking me or telling me?" Tadgh asked, voice dangerously even.

"Asking," I said, heart aching. "Always asking."

He nodded, and that was that.

"And you Niamh? Will the Boirinn stand with the Macha and the Muir?"

"Well," Niamh said, clearing their throat. "There is something that could persuade me."

"Persuade you," I echoed. "More than the preservation of all tuath?"

"Yes," they said, and barreled ahead. "Even before this….situation… I've carried a shadow."

"It's a curse, dear," Caoimhe said quietly. "Let's call a spade a spade."

"Fine, a *curse*," Niamh acknowledged.

I looked at Tadhg but he shrugged. I sighed. "What's the curse? Tell me it's not more poetry. I've had enough with poetry tonight, I think."

Niamh shook their head. "No, not especially. Just that even before this situation became clearly…what it is…I shouldn't bring about a child."

I couldn't connect the dots. "I don't understand."

"Why not?" Tadhg asked.

"Well, this is awkward really, but—"

"Your mother, Tadhg," Caoimhe cut in. "She's the one who cursed them. 'May your fire dim when your get becomes a parent,' or some such. During the war."

"Rude of her," Tadhg said. "But very in character."
"What are you asking?" Kandace asked and Caoimhe jumped, almost as if she'd forgotten Kandace was there.

"We can't have a child together, for fear it will invoke the curse. They want—"

Niamh held up a hand and spoke formally: "If you promise this will be the end of the darkness that eats away at the future of our Courts, for the aid of Boirinn, we ask for comhar with Gaita, bound in saol. The fruits of which will go to Boirinn and Gaita. To be carried by the light of the New Moon."

"Now wait *one* moment," Tadhg said.

I cocked my head. "If this was about securing your line, you could ask for the saol of anyone. But you want Gaita bound to the Macha. Why?"

"Where's Thahliah, Baird?" Caoimhe's voice went ice cold.

"What?" Now I was even more confused. "Your sister? I certainly don't know."

Caoimhe held my gaze for a moment and then nodded, the ice thawing. "I believe you. But the *first* thing I would do after this mess is done, if there is comhar between our Courts, is ask *your* sister where mine is. And why the last sign I've seen of her is an invitation to your sister's estate."

I couldn't speak for Maeve. I remembered that conversation we had in the steam room. *I've already handled the Gaita,* she'd said. There were plenty of things that she did on behalf of the Court that I knew little of. "I—I didn't know."

Tadhg crossed his arms across his chest and jerked his head to the side. I stepped away with him. He spoke quietly and furiously. "If you do this wretched thing, and Maeve will kill you for it—mark my words, she will be after a murder *as soon as she hears of it*—but if you do it, you will give her saol for three children, not two. And one of them is *mine.*" We both breathed heavy into the silence that followed. "And if you don't give me that, we are done. Our comhar is over."

"Tadhg—what? We've never even *talked* of a child." I was reeling.

"You and I haven't, no. Because you're never fecking *there*, Baird. Ask your sister and she would let you know exactly how much it means to me."

"But Tadhg, I would be a terrible father. A dreadful one. And that is the *last* thing I can do. Cern being awful is part of how we even got to this place."

Tadhg turned away, still clutching himself. "I'm warning you, Baird. If you give that tuath saol for young ones, but not one for me, we are done for."

"This is—oh, for feck's sake, Tadhg. You're honestly going to blackmail me into making a *baby*?" My volume see-sawed as I tried to stay reasonable.

"Is it blackmail, or is it taking advantage of a jackpot? This is the one time I've ever heard Baird mac Macha even *considering* a child, so, I'm making my intentions known."

It didn't add up. "But... you could make a baby with Maeve."

Tadgh's eyebrows flew into his hair. "Just...make one with Maeve, he says. Baird, I don't just want *any* baby. I want your baby. And I want *you* to want a baby." He was crying now, but he wouldn't let me touch him. He stormed off down the path.

"This is a mess," I said, kneeling and pressing my palm into my eyes. I felt a hand on my shoulder. I turned and Kandace stood there. We shared a moment, unease and pain and friendship held in the space between us.

"Alright then?" she asked.

Niamh and Caoimhe both looked at me uncertainly.

"That...didn't seem to go well," Niamh said.

Caoimhe's face twinged at Niamh's words; not how she would have said it, I guessed, but I appreciated their forthrightness.

I shook my palm back and forth. "So so," I said.

Caoimhe's face didn't really change, but Niamh clapped me on the back, their other hand firmly pushed into the fur of Kells, who now looked a hare the size of a pony.

I didn't see a way through this besides doing what everyone wanted. I needed them to confront Cern. I sighed, a big whoosh of air. "I pledge comhar to the Court of the Gaita, as one of the Macha's children. Let it be known by our young."

I leaned into my power, the saol of the Court, and pulled it thick and strong into the air around us. The Macha manifested with the smell of earth, rich loam, along with an unequivocal centering, a gravitas made of rock that filled us. A single raven roosted on the wall, their eye wicked and knowing. Caoimhe had been taken off guard, but she called the Gaita too, and though the moon was waxing, so close to their home, it gleamed austere and cunning, cutting through the clouds for its mistress. The air grew thick with secrets and Caoimhe's glamour flared, such that a spasm of longing went through me and Niamh's fingers clutched inchoately at Caoimhe's hair, frustrated with yearning. These would be the legacies that these younglings would draw on, no matter what Court they were given to. I held out my palms to Caoimhe and my saol rushed into my hands. When the Gaita's saol did the same, I *twisted* with three deft motions, until a trio of coruscating pearls gleamed amidst our fingers. Then it was done, and I let the Macha dissipate, the effort of holding it there turning my spine into jelly.

I knelt, exhausted, and looked up. Caoimhe looked just as tired, but she peered at the pearls of saol in confusion. "Three?" she asked.

Before I could answer, Tadhg embraced me, his long tresses wild and getting into my eye. I tried to push him off heart-heartedly, but I couldn't. Over his shoulder, Tadhg said, "One for Gaita, one for Boirinn, and one for the Macha."

Surprised, I said, "I thought, perhaps, for the Muir, but..."

"That wasn't what we agreed on," Niamh said, testing to see if Caoimhe would agree with them.

But Caoimhe shook her head, slowly. "This is fine. One for Gaita, one for Boirinn, and one for the Macha."

Kandace looked at Caoimhe with skepticism. "You're going to be big as a house."

Tadhg smiled at Kandace. "Not how it'll work, chicken, not this time."

Niamh frowned at the pearls, nervous despite themselves. "You'll need to protect them, until we fix this thing. No knowing what might happen if you release them too soon."

"I'll be fine. This is fine," Caimhe said again. A slow smile started to wend its way across her face, but the papers that Niamh had collected off Kells put her back into the present. "Kandace, will you stay with me, and do more research on your warding spell, while these three head off into danger?"

"Oh, am I allowed now?" Kandace's eyebrow flew up.

Caoimhe shrugged. "Apparently, you were in the library the whole time," she said, tapping the likeness of Kandace on the page, cradling the pearls of saol against her chest.

"Do you have a kettle in there somewhere?"

"I'd be a fool to think you'd stay otherwise, wouldn't I? Of course I do. Come on with you." Caoimhe gestured towards the cliff.

"Baird, catch," was all my warning before Kandace's keys thwacked into my chest. "Don't bang up my car."

I snorted. "As if you'd notice."

"Just be careful, okay?"

"Of course, I will. Will have it back to you in a jiff, honest."

"That's not what I meant, and you know it."

I tipped an imaginary hat at my only friend in the world. "Got it, your majesty."

"I'm going to murder you."

"Please murder him later," Caoimhe asked, linking arms with Kandace. "We have research to do."

Niamh kissed Caoimhe goodbye such that I think all of our cheeks went hot. The púca might even have whined. "My love."

Tadhg plucked the keys from my hand as soon as they

walked away, Caoimhe's heels still echoing on the paving stones.

"Hey," I said. "She gave them to me."

"Baird, you don't know how to drive."

My mouth opened and closed. It was true.

"Shotgun," Niamh said.

"Back seat right side," I said. Tadhg snorted.

"Kells will keep you company." Niamh's chipperness could become a problem, I decided.

As they got into the car, something whined from some bushes nearby. It made the hair on the back of my neck prickle. I crept towards the bush, wondering if I would be attacked again. White teeth gaped at me, a pink tongue—just as I might have shouted for aid, I glimpsed a weary wagging tail and my eyes ached.

Poor Jenny. She was littered with wounds, her belly a seeping mess. The hunger had left her, as soon it didn't need her. The dog licked at my face, all the while whining with pain.

"You good girl, Jenny. You're such a good girl. The best girl," I said, over and over again, scratching behind her ears and looking for the bit of light inside her that gave her life. It was a thin and wretched thing, barely there. The cruelest gift of the Macha, the ease with which we could cut a mortal life short. Not a gift I welcomed.

"You are the best girl. Good girl, Jenny." She could not survive. I knew that. So I snuffed her out.

They called my name while I threw up into the bushes.

I emptied my stomach until it held nothing but bile, steeled myself, and headed back to the car.

he ride passed with almost buoyant camaraderie and small talk until we saw the stain on the sky. Amidst the clouds, and the grey, and the sliver of robin's egg blue, the overcast sky over Westmeath looked bruised. Deep purples and sullen black greens where it should have been opalescent and gleaming.

"Is that right?" Niamh asked, hoping that one of us would reassure them.

"Ah sure, it will be after we leave, won't it? Not a bother," I said.

Niamh didn't look reassured.

Kells turned out to be a remarkably good cuddler in the backseat, head resting on my thigh and big doleful eyes. "How'd you end up with this tuath, huh?" I asked the púca idly.

"He lost a wrestling match," Niamh said, their chin jutting up with pride.

"With you?" Tadhg's pitch jumped up with surprise.

"Is anyone else telling you this story?" Niamh's feelings sounded hurt. "Yeah, with me."

"While it changed the whole time? Fair play to you."

I tuned them out when Niamh started going through the play by play. Kells's head popped up during the recitation so

I gave the púca a mollifying pat until it settled down. I had a missed call and a voice mail from Fea, probably wondering why the saol had gotten just a bit thinner. *This mess will be over shortly, I suspect. Let's chat later today*, I texted her. She'd probably be in a better mood with me after I sorted out this Cern issue.

When we arrived at the base of the hill, the stain completely covered the sky. Like we were inside the bruise, which seemed about right.

The pub was already open, which raised my eyebrows. "Will we have Guinness for breakfast?" I suggested, and with no objections, we headed inside. Kells waited in the car, Niamh's hand a light touch at my elbow.

The bartender didn't remark on the time, or dwell on us especially, just poured our pints, waited for them to settle, and poured the rest. The lack of attention raised my hackles. The three of us were *exquisite*. He should be wrapped around our finger. When he turned to clean glasses, I mouthed "Marked?" to Tadhg and he made a face at me like it should be obvious. Which maybe I would have remembered if the last time I'd been here, I hadn't been busy sobbing on Fea.

I suspected that meant that Cern would not be surprised by our arrival. In any case, we kept our conversation to a minimum, paid and left. Kells waited outside the pub, curled into a circle of white fluff that looked mostly doglike. "I thought we left the púca in the car..." I said.

Niamh snickered. "How often have you said that?" They pushed their hand into the ruff of white fur to give Kells a good scritch.

Tadgh stood at the edge of the parking lot, hands on his hips, a breeze coming off the hill turning his hair and scarf into an anime gif. A spear half again as tall as him glittered in his hand, and I imagined that the loo was now missing a mirror. He looked over his shoulder at us. "Will we get on with it?"

Niamh and I fell in beside him and heading up the hill, Boirinn's fire in Niamh's hand and my war hammer at the ready. My feet fell more sure on the earth, shod this time, perhaps still remembering the way to the peak, but there were differences from last time. The small creatures that had been alive with sound and movement, comfortable with the tread of tuath, were quiet. Had Ethliu's Hunger been unable to contain itself from feasting upon her favorites? That would bode poorly for her restraint.

A text on the way up from Kandace: *Caoimhe found another text with my face in it, linking me to Ethliu. I can almost remember how to make one of these scrolls. I KNOW I've done it before. But I think I need Ethliu's name. Her real name.*

I texted back: *I'll try and get it. We're headed up the hill now.*

The silence meant that when the leaves above us rustled with movement, it didn't feel like an overreaction for the three of us to jump back, tense with the presence of impending violence. A dead raven fell between us, twist of paper in its beak, a grim summons. My heart clenched as Tadhg bent down. "Who?" I asked, but he shook his head.

"Court tonight," he said, glancing skyward. "Plenty of

time for us to have news to share."

Niamh crossed their muscled arms over their chest and inclined their head. "Cuirim onóir do theach."

"I suppose there's nothing to do but keep heading up," I said, sighing. "Be ready for the ward stones at the stop. They'll show you things. The past, I think, but I'm not sure." I told them a little about what they'd showed me, just the bare bones of it. And sure enough, we found the cleft in the stone.

I remembered something. "Last time, when I came to, I was inside the keep. With Cern and Fea. Perhaps, if we were to enter while linked, we might be less vulnerable to the hill's whims." I slung my war hammer to my belt and extended my hands to each of them, such that Niamh could still keep their other hand on Kells and Tadhg could do the same with his spear. The two nodded and we clasped hands, stepping through without further discussion.

Or so I imagined. I remembered making that decision, and the careful step forward, but then I was falling, and my two companions were lost to me.

"What do you reckon?" Maeve asked, pudgy hands balled at her waist, face smudged with dirt.

I felt cold, down here in the hole we'd dug, despite the fair day that I knew was up beyond the lip of the grave. "They're right where the shadow girl said they'd be," I said.

Maeve ducked down to inspect the bones, unwilling to keep digging with the shovel now that we'd found something. She pulled the sleeve of her jumper over her hand and wiped away at them. They'd been blackened by fire, yes but also carved, covered with writing.

"What do they say?" I asked, knowing what Maeve would say.

"It's the same thing over and over," she said, uncovering another line of glyphs. "Devourer, our lady, take Brenna mac Ethliu to your breast, and give us Spring."

It said "Devourer," like the same word we'd use for finishing a meal, but it was a name, I knew it was. And the way Maeve said it made me feel even colder.

"So—you saw what she wrote. That means…" I trailed off.

"They killed her," Maeve said, voice flat.

"W-we—" I stuttered, my teeth chattering. "We have to do something about this."

"Yes," came the baritone reply, from above the pit. Above the grave. "Yes, we do."

Strong arms hooked under my armpits. Maeve screamed and pulled at me, but Cern was too strong. He pulled me up, legs twisting, and Maeve followed, the two of us a wild beast of scratching fingers and kicking feet. Had we ever felt fear like that before? It was hard to remember. But the emotion made us dig our heels into our powers, and the Court of the Macha manifested around us, the earth reminding us that we were her children, and that the scion of Ethliu had no power to move us while we were close to her.

Maeve held an acorn in her hand, one she'd found in her pocket— we'd spent the morning by the creek, swimming and lobbing them at each other—and did more than just use the power of the Court to stand her ground. She stole a little of the Macha's saol and funnelled it into the seed, such that even as Maeve threw it in the grave, the acorn was splitting, and a green sapling jutting out.

When Cern returned, Fea beside him to drag the wayward children indoors, the grave had already been filled and the oak's branches spread over us. He sighed when he recognized it. "Here's another thing you can't remember," he said, and I screamed, because I didn't want to forget—

"Baird, it's okay. We made it. Baird, we're here." Niamh knelt beside me, Kells licking at my face, while Tadhg had his spear leveled at something away from us. The sun had moved more than it should; hours must have passed.

"We have to do something about this," I said, eyes going flinty, spine pulling deep on the earth to right myself. In my hand, something small and hard—an acorn. The discovery of it made me want to cry.

"Yes, we do," Niamh said, their voice hard as well.

That name. *Devourer*, in the old language. I texted it to Kandace, phonetically. *Caoimhe will know how to spell it*, I sent in a second text. But I had no bars...I had no idea if they would send.

Tadhg coughed. "When you're ready, Baird. Get up, will you?"

I put my phone away and pushed myself up, still scattered and unaware of my surroundings. "I saw Brenna. I know it's all true, now. Are you two alright?"

"This path can't show me anything worse than what has already happened to me," Tadhg said, a challenge. That was when I realized, truly, that we weren't alone. Tadhg's spear, shining and deadly, pointed at Cern, who waited patiently and securely, surrounded by a host of animals, their fur serrated and inky, suserating with Ethliu's Hunger. Behind him, mounted on a plinth, a massive war shield containing the ashes of a fire, massed with heather, sea aster and fragrant juniper.

"I always forget that he's so *beautiful*," Tadhg sighed. It took me off guard. I don't remember a time when I beheld Cern for himself alone, and not the father who'd been such a disappointment. But I supposed it was true, he was a vision, even among tuath. He'd dressed in diaphanous white silks today, slit here and there to expose his chest and his well-turned calves, a heavy black wool cloak making an elegant backdrop to the ensemble. His features were a balanced juxtaposition of easy ruggedness—the esteemed badgerlike pelt of his chest and the muscled bulk of his shoulders—with captivating grace—the fine architecture of his face, the coquettish lean of his hips.

"Hello, my child. Glad to have you back for a visit." Cern could have been having us over for brunch. "You're always welcome here, you know. But I'd love it if you gave me a bell before bringing visitors."

"I'm hardly a visitor, Da," Tadhg said, throwing a twee country accent on for size, his voice bitter and clipped. "Although I suppose I've only been family for a ré or so."

"This can't go on, Cern. We have to put a stop to it." My declaration came out more wistful than I would have liked.

Cern shook his head, ignoring me. "Perhaps I've been wrong, Tadhg. I wrote you off too soon. What would it take for you to stand beside me?"

Tadhg's face fell into a frown. "Are you bargaining with

me?"

Cern gestured to the amassed abominations that encircled us. "Would it hurt to listen? Or must you stoop right away to bloodshed like Glenn."

"What does this have to do with Glenn?" I yelled.

"I'm not talking to you, Baird."

Tadhg looked at me but I shrugged; he would need to decide this for himself.

"Ethliu is strong," Cern said. "And this keep would give you space away from the endless bickering of the Macha. You would be beholden to one but yourself. No sisters, no feckless consort, no endless worrying about comhar."

Cern's words as he unfolded this offer felt like a slap in the face, chilling and disrespectful, but Tadhg's response froze me solid: "You don't know me well enough, Cern. Why not offer to solve my real problem? Seems you're not as insightful as you think."

Cern stared at Tadhg, as if hoping that Tadhg might break and say what this real problem might be, but my consort had been studied by eyes more astute than Cern's, and he did not crack.

So he turned to Niamh. "What about the child of the Boirinn, bearer of the Muir's curse? My lady manifests first in those that bear her duality. Amongst the Boirinn, you will forever be the unlucky child, but in Ethliu's Court, you would displace even me."

Niamh kept silent, listening. The only thing betraying their tension was the whiteness of their knuckles in Kells' fur.

Cern held up his arm and a winged shape from the trees swooped down to alight on his forearm, its sharp talons gouging bloody rents in his skin, though he did not cry out. "The small things in the trees are my eyes, wild and many. You'd never step uncertain through the world again."

This prompted Niamh's laugh. "You stumble, mac Ethliu."

"He's not mac Ethliu," I say, a reminder. "He is mac Riven. Father, I ask you again, what did you do to Glenn?"

Cern cut the air with his hand like a knife, the bird pushing itself away from him and into the bruised sky with a buffeting of wind. "Fea would have told you that if she'd wanted to. And it is no longer relevant. Ethliu supplants all. What about you, my child? You are my greatest joy, you know. Your sister is a tribute to your mother and Fea, but you, I will happily claim."

I made a wretching, disbelieving scoff, deep in my throat. "You expect me to believe that? I can't remember the last time I heard something so false."

"Why would I lie?" Cern asked, with that voice. A bit tougher, more gristle, but still velvet. "Look at you. You are the rock that a child of the Muir dashed his ship across, well-made and virile. You make of your life what you will, no matter the machinations of your family. You stand alone, and beg their notice. I couldn't be more proud. You would be a prize for Ethliu, Baird. An absolute prize." He opened his arms to me, and I wanted to feel like a child again, to throw myself there. "Come Baird, join me. Forget all this."

But the talk of forgetting fell like a bucket of water over my head. Memory assailed me, and I felt it like the first time, him trying to pull from that grave, the bones of my sister at my feet. No. No, I would not go. I opened my mouth to say so when the words from Caoimhe's text rang in my head.

Thrice denied, once reclaimed. Horror dawned in me. Did he *want* us to rebuke him?

I stepped closer, ignoring Tadhg's gasp.

"Baird, what about—" I ignored Niamh and stepped forward again.

Cern's expression couldn't be harder to read. His arms wavered, but stayed open. Surprised, yes, but disconcerted. "So much of my life has been driven by obligation, by necessity, but you shone through despite that. My shining son. How it pained me that she claimed you. You should have taken the name I coveted. I would have been so proud to call you Baird mac Ethliu."

I moaned and stepped forward again. I couldn't help it. What punishment was this, to hear such kindness at a moment like this? Real tears blinded me. But Cern couldn't stop the poison from coming out of his mouth. I knew what would have happened if I hadn't been promised to the Macha. My bones would be black from fire in an unmarked grave beside the sister I never knew.

"Baird, what the feck are you *doing*?" Tadhg shouted, and I realized that Cern and I had *both* lost concentration. Niamh and Tadhg were back to back, surrounded by the creatures possessed by Ethliu's hunger.

"All my life——" I cut myself off with a quiet sob. I stumbled forward again. Cern's pulse jumped visibly in his neck, he reached back to steady himself against the plinth. If I reached out, we could embrace. But I couldn't do that. I started over. "For decades, no, for a ré, I wondered what I could have done differently. How I could have earned your trust, but——"

I noticed that the shield behind Cern contained not only flowers and wood as I'd thought, but bones, blackened and charred. Some were old and dry, but others were… fresh. A glint within the pile caught my eye. A silver flash.

"There was nothing you could have done, Baird." Cern sounded defeated. "I kept you away on purposes. How could I ask you to be my kin when the only inheritance I had to offer was made of bones and an unslakable hunger."

I squinted harder at the pile, the silver jewelry. It took my eyes too long to make sense of the shape. Four legs, a flowing mane… a horse. A silver horse. When I realized its nature, I fell to my knees. The raven this morning, summoning us to Court. The Macha who had died—it was Fea. And Cern had killed her.

Cern bent down to hold me, self-loathing written all over his face. "Baird——"

"You *monster*! I would *never* join you!" I barrelled into him, knocking my head against his chest and throwing him down. My fist careened into my father's face, once, splitting my knuckles, twice, breaking his nose. But the next punch I threw at him met with his upraised hand, and the presence that looked back at me from Cern's eyes was cold, ancient, and hungry. Ethliu, manifesting in my father's skin, threw me off of her like a ragdoll.

Of course—the third denial. I'd handed it to her on a plate. And yes, there were the signs of Ethliu's Court manifesting—I hadn't noticed them at first. The air, dark and warm, like a cave, like the inside of a womb. The trees, and her possessed creatures, seething with bristling life. And the hunger that ran through my body like a lifetime of famine.

"What's happening?" Niamh asked. Kells slumped down, struggling to move. The púca may have been immortal and fey, but it was not tuath. A possessed stoat sunk its teeth into Niamh's calf before they could sear it with the undying fire of the Boirinn.

"Focus," Tadhg said, spinning like a dancer, the length of his spear black with blood. "They do not weary."

He was right; the creatures were emboldened, their hunger amplified.

Ethliu stood, and it horrified me to see how completely she possessed Cern's flesh. Where Cern had carried himself gracefully, still, he walked like tuath. Ethliu stalked like a wildcat, a beast that hadn't been seen in Eire for decades. The black hunger within the beasts filled Ethliu now too, darkening her veins to ink and seeping from her temples like a mane of rotten shadow. Ethliu flung her head back and howled. The presence of her Court reverberated around her as she gathered its strength to her.

I reeled back, clutching the war hammer. The sky had

darkened behind Ethliu's bruised clouds, and I knew that the long slide into evening loomed upon us. The Macha's court would be manifesting soon. If we lived long enough, perhaps I could summon it here.

Unfortunately, not all the Ethliu's hungers were weasels and stoats; now Tadhg danced with a beast so large it could only be a bear. If anyone had asked me if there were still bears alive on Eire, I would have hesitated. After this night, I suspect they will all be dead. The beast glistened darkly from a dozen wounds, but still it swiped at my consort with awful claws. I thought to lend him my aid, but in a motion that stirred poetry in my unlyrical heart, Tadhg threw himself beneath the beast and thrust upward. I dashed closer and shoved at the bear's corpse to prevent it from falling on him. He nodded at me, his hair drenched with sweat, and flew towards Ethliu with his spear.

Niamh appeared much less certain without Kells at their side; now forced to defend their friend as well as themself, their fire burned less often, and I feared they would flag. I rallied myself beside them, poor Kells between us so that they could pay more attention to our attackers. My arm swung the hammer over and over, crushing bones and fending off wild things, fatigue grinding into my muscles with each swing.

"Baird!"

It took a moment for me to recognize Kandace's voice amidst this fray. When had she arrived? She carried her whip, but Ethliu's Court already took its toll on her. "It's too dangerous," I said. "You need to go." I pivoted and swung my hammer. A possessed fox's ribs crunched; it made an awful whine as it died. A boar took its place. There were so many of them.

"I can't," she said. "I have to do this. I have to get closer to Tadhg. Niamh…"

"Go," they said, panting. Niamh's fists were alight with their fire, but they were exhausted. "I'm not dead yet, am I?"

"No, first—" Kandace fought through her exhaustion. "A signal flare. Can you do that? I left my phone with the driver. She needs to tell Caoimhe—oh feck." She slumped over, her complexion sweaty and sallow.

I stood over my friend as Niamh gathered their strength, invigorated by their lover's name. They pushed their forearms together and spread their fingers up towards the sky, gritting their teeth to force a billowing plume of flame cloudward, such that for a moment it obliterated the sight of Ethliu's bruise. Even Ethliu, who had turned a gnarled branch into a staff and partnered Tadhg in his awful dance, paused to look at the flame.

"What happens?" I asked Kandace, swinging my hammer to keep black claws away. "*Something needs to happen.*"

"Feck it, Caoimhe. *Come on,*" I heard Kandace whisper.

The seconds ticked, terrible and fruitless, our reserves dwindling and the awful beasts unending. Until the wind shifted, and I tasted salt. I saw Tadhg's strength buoy, and knew it was the sea. As one, the hungry beasts lifted their heads, as if to some unseen call, and then they stampeded to the east, in a raucous melange of shrieks and cries and bellows.

"Thank you, Caoimhe," Kandace said to the earth. "Thank you."

"What…" I didn't even know what to ask, I just offered Kandace my hand, now that there were no fell beasts to avert.

"The sea is too great for her to drink," she quoted. "Caoimhe's idea. We used those bloody rags from the *second* time you were attacked to make a lure of sorts. Caoimhe has set it in the sea."

"I can't pretend to understand, but I'm grateful nonetheless."

Kandace sketched a dismissive gesture. "We all play our part." Kandace leaned on me hard and couldn't stand on her own.

The night tightened her grip on the day even as we spoke, and I felt the subtle pressure of obligation that let me know that the Court demanded to manifest. Yet Ethliu's grip on this place was too tight. The Macha couldn't arrive while Ethliu was looking. Not out in the open.

I thought of the clearing inside the keep. The oak tree that bore vigil to my sister, that held within it a tiny bit of Maeve's young saol. "Come," I said. "We must hurry."

I dragged Kandace more than anything else, and Niamh called out to us as we ran, but I didn't have time to explain. No time to ask Tadhg to hold on just a bit longer. No time at all. The tree, with my conflicting memories of it dueling in my head now, shone like a beacon. And the Macha's insistence grew here, away from Ethliu's dominance.

"Oh," Kandace said. A small sound of wonder, when a stone table appeared in our midst, dwarfing the tiny children's table that I'd once played with. And seated there, Granddame, Maeve, and Ciara. My heart was speared anew to see my cousin where my aunt should be. I hadn't been wrong. Fea was gone.

As my family became more solid, I turned my attention back to the tree. That oak that bore witness to my sister's fate. I could not make Kandace one with the Macha, but I could imbue her with our strength, for a little while. For long enough to do this right. "Come here," I said, reaching out to her with one hand, and the tree with the other. I didn't give her time to object. I took the tree's life, the rich skein that had been born by Maeve's saol and the leftover strength of our sister, and I wrenched it loose. Even as the tree perished, the cellulose of it aging so rapidly that it became ash, I wove that cord of life around Kandace's like cable around a wire. *I'm sorry, Brenna.*

Maeve screamed in outrage, and flew at me with a black blade extended, one of our mother's. "Go," I said to Kandace. "To Tadgh." And I heaved up the stone table we'd sat at as children to fend off my sister while Kandace fled.

"Maeve, no!"

The uncanny black knife gouged a rent in the marble, a feat I would have questioned if I hadn't heard the tales of my mother's blades. Maeve snarled, inchoate with anger. I was lucky that the Three had not yet manifested, or nothing would have saved me. Maeve must have realized the same, because she turned back towards the others. Ciara looked at me with wide eyes. Granddame's gaze was implacable and fathomless.

I'd given Kandace enough time, I thought. I dropped the table and ran back towards Ethliu, only now truly seeing the number of twisted beasts that lay dead and dying across the field. Tadhg and Ethliu still danced, but slower now. Tadhg had scored Ethliu's shoulder, a great wound that left Cern's bone and meat exposed to the air. But Ethliu seemed to care little for her host's frailties, and even Tadhg's legendary constitution could not last forever.

Kandace cleared her throat, on the edge of their dangerous motion. "Stop this, *Devourer*. At once." Her voice rang out like a bell, Ethliu's old name clunky and strange in Kandace's North Dublin cadences.

Ethliu fell back as if punched, so Kadence called out again. "Begone, *Devourer*. You are not welcome here."

The bruise in the sky wavered like a mirage as she yelled. The Court's manifestation wavered, and the terrible pulse that drummed though us faltered.

Ethliu howled, Kandace's voice paining her, and she pulled away from Tadhg.

Kandace still yelled: "*Devourer*, I name you, and *Devourer*, I banish you!"

Ethliu's jaw unhinged and widened, mouth filled with impossible black teeth, and I thought that we'd made a mistake, that Kandace's sovereignty would not be recognized.

She hurled herself at Kandace. I grabbed Kandace's arm, yanking her backwards, but she would not budge. But as Ethliu's jaws would have closed on Kandace's face, Tadhg's spear scoured Ethliu again, a brutal wound to the back.

"Devourer, by my word begone!" Kandace cried for a final time, face to face with the ancient goddess.

With a clap of soundless thunder, she banished Ethliu from my father's dying body. Her Court vanished, as if it had never been.

he hillside became alive once more. The song of the nightjar rose and fell and joined the drumming of snipe wings, the tireless croaking of corncrakes. The Macha crept and stretched over the keep, growing and thriving as the pent up saol that Ethliu had stolen returned to us. I breathed it in, eyes cast towards the stars, and thought of Fea. She was part of us again. I could feel her. And not just our own—this salt on the wind, the saol of the Muir. This smoky tongue of fire, the saol of the Boirinn. Tadhg and Niamh stood a bit taller in its glow, but mostly, the Macha took the returned saol as its due.

I waited for something else, too. Surely Caoimhe would notice, even from afar—yes. I signaled to Kandace, the only one I trusted to help me break my news without meddling. She disappeared into the keep. The shards of saol Caoimhe and I had made together, forged of intention, were no longer held in abeyance, waiting for the right time. I felt them, and knew there would be young ones amidst the tuath once again.

If it weren't for this chaos, this unheard of strength that ran through us all, the others would have felt it too. But as of yet, in the midst of this strangeness, it was still my secret to tell.

Granddame's hand fell on my shoulder, fine-veined and venerable. I shied away from her grip, even as she praised me. "You surprised me, Baird. This wasn't a future I saw for us."

"You knew." Just those words. Said without emotion. But still—an accusation. That I'd dared to say to the most powerful of the Macha. "How could—"

"There will be reckoning from this day, Baird. But you will not be the one to bring it to bear. Do you understand?" Granddame did not bother to hide her steel. I understood her plainly. If I expected an apology, or an explanation, I would not get it. But she would not reprimand me when she discovered my new secret. Not when I'd freed us from the burden of her decisions.

"By your leave," I said, tongue somehow not acid, and left her there.

And good timing I had, since Niamh had been approaching my sister, who stood by the plinth with my cousin Ciara. "I know," I said quietly to them. "But not yet."

"When—"

I didn't let them finish. I stood between them and gestured towards the shield bearing the remnants of Ethliu's offerings.

Louder, I said, "Niamh, I wanted to ask you. Can you—" I stopped, unable to say the words. I knew that what remained there but just remnants, now that her saol had been brought back to us, but still. It felt right.

Niamh steadied themselves on Kells and brought the undying fire of the Boirinn onto the remaining bones. The smell of juniper joined the salt and smoke on the breeze. The fire drew the attention of the whole Court, and I seized the moment and raised my voice. "Cousins, consort, and the Three, I have an announcement." I paused, and slightly quieter, asked. "Wait, where *is* my consort?"

The crowd laughed awkwardly while I searched the crowd. I looked around for Tadhg. I would have wanted to have him beside me for this. But still. "There is much to mourn today," I said, my voice breaking, surprising myself by aching for not only Fea, but Cern. "And mourn we shall, with food and drink. But not only that."

At the sound of drink, Kandace came out with two trays of wine, acquired from the keep's cellars. I took one from her and we distributed them, until every hand held a glass. "There is also something to celebrate. Though some of you might be surprised, not least of all my dear Tadhg, I'm to be a father."

And in the surprised cheering that followed, where Granddame's face might actually have split open from joy, and Maeve's twisted in surprise, I shouted. "Here's to my children and the comhar with the Gaita that brought them to me."

The cheering carried on, even as Maeve's surprise became dread. I found myself back to Niamh's side. "Wait until she comes to you," I suggested. "She'll bring up Thahliah right away."

"We'll see," they said, and when I would have spoken again, they put a strong hand over my mouth. "I swear by the fire, Baird. If you cut me off one more time, I will thrash you."

I felt a pique of irritation, but they weren't wrong. I kept my mouth shut, abashed.

"Thank you," they said. "That's all. Thank you."

I gripped their hand in mine. What else would I say? No, thank *you*? Words were meaningless sometimes. I hated this feeling. Usually I only felt it around Tadhg. Unconsciously, I twisted around looking for him.

"You lost Tadhg, didn't know?" Niamh asked. "Last I saw him, he was down the hill, by the maple grove."

I thanked them and hurried off, snatching two glasses of wine from the tray. I marveled that he should have sought solace in the same place that I had during my last visit last.

It was quieter down the hill, with half the keep between us and the revelry. An owl hooted, or perhaps a dove. I'd never been able to tell the difference. Tadhg had perched himself up on a lip of crumbling stone wall, looking down the hill towards the town far below. My footsteps weren't quiet, but he didn't look back at me.

"Mind some company?" I called up.

"No," his words drifted down. "I don't mind."

I put the glasses on the wall first, and then heaved myself up. My sore muscles shouted at me, and I managed to knock over a bit of loose shale. I was panting by the time I settled next to him. "Feck's sake, Tadhg. You didn't pick an easy place to sit."

Tadhg met my eye, and I found myself quietly relieved by the expression there. He looked melancholy, yes, but not furious. He pointed a languid hand to the right, where I now realized a ladder had been welded into the stone. "I nearly told you but then I was enjoying myself too much," he confessed.

I grumbled, but let it go, instead holding out one of my glasses to him. "Cheers," I said.

He took it and clinked it against mine by instinct, seeming to regret it right after. He sipped and then sighed. "What are we drinking to, Baird? Another ré of being awful to each other?"

The complaint felt small to me, after all we'd just been through, but I let that flow through me. I didn't know what to say. I rested my head on his shoulders, my eyes against the pillow of his sweet-smelling hair. I inhaled, long and hard, before I started. "Why do you smell so good? You just murdered a goddess in single combat."

"Well, I—" Tadhg stumbled, caught.

I went in for the kill. "You took a *bath*, didn't you? You missed my whole bloody speech because you were taking a bath. I can't believe it."

"There was so much blood I—"

I couldn't help it, I just started laughing. And soon enough, Tadhg was laughing too. A real laugh, the kind that left us both crying and threatened to drop our wine, or even us, from the wall. He ended up clutching me for balance, wiped at his eyes with his sleeve. "See," I said. "We still know how to laugh."

Tadhg inhaled, stilling his objections. "We do," he said finally. "Clearly we do."

"Maybe that can be enough. For now." I put my arm around my consort. "That and the baby."

"The baby," Tadhg echoed. "We're going to have a baby." He made another sound, and it took me a moment to understand that he was sobbing.

"What, love? I thought you'd be happy." I put down my wine so that I could hold him with both arms. Tadhg shook against me.

"I am. I promise. It just feels so wrong to be this happy without Fea. I'd always wanted to make her proud."

My eyes shone with unshed tears, thinking about the vision that was Tadhg mac Muir and his silver spear dueling with the *Devourer* of Ethliu, so that the tuath's dead might once again be one with their people. "She's proud of you, love. I promise. I am too."

We sat on the wall, just breathing, until Tadhg remembered his wine and downed it. I followed suit. "Let's head back," he said.

I jumped down, thrilling in the moment between wall and ground where the earth didn't hold me. It was a good feeling. I looked up at Tadhg and held out my arms with a grin, grunting when he jumped into them. I was ready to fall in love with him all over again.

Falling felt like anything could happen.

onths later, Tadgh and I broke our fast at sunset on a hilltop in Cork, leaning up against the rowan tree that had borne witness to so many of Fea and Glenn's poorly hidden assignations. Fitting that it now grew the young tuath that would be our child.

"Give us your phone, will you?" Tadhg asked.

"What for?" I asked, handing it over and rifling through the things Tadhg had brought for us to eat.

"You look a bit handsome, with the sun and all. Jaysus, Baird, do you ever check your voicemails?"

"People know to text me if it's important." Something occurred to me as I stuffed gouda into my face. "Have you been hanging around Kandace? I've don't think you've ever said *jaysus* before in your life."

"We have a bit of a chat here and there," Tadhg said, still rifling through my phone. "And I know *I've* certainly left you voicemails without texting. How many have you just—oh."

"Love, I'm sorry, you know that I—"

"No, Baird, look. There's one from Fea. The day that—"

"What?" I asked. "Give me that."

Tadhg was right. I remembered texting her that nonsense

about everything being fine. I wanted to listen to it, and I didn't. What if she'd asked me for help? And I'd ignored her?

"Go on," Tadhg said. "Put it on speaker. I really need to hear her voice."

I exhaled, long and hard, but I did what he said, then held the phone between our ears so we could hear it. The phone hissed something awful, and made whushing noises that I didn't understand.

"What is it?" I asked over the sound.

Tadhg cackled. "I think it's a butt dial.

It whuffed and screeched a little while longer, and then two words from Fea: "Damn this sodding thing."

"Typical," I said. "She hated that piece of shite mobile she carried around."

Tadhg pulled me close, and I called the saol of the Macha to us, solid and warm. It wasn't the same as holding her, but it was as close as I could get. I put my hand against the rowan tree, and felt the wee light within it press up against my fingers. They'd be with us in a year or so, saol willing.

"Little thing, if you have the smallest scrap of Fea mac Macha's ill humour, you will be well loved."

"They'll get plenty of that from you," Tadhg muttered.

"Hush," I said. "I'm charming."

Tadgh snorted and laid his fingers over mine. "Yes, love. Sure you are."

We finished the bits of jam and bread and cheese, getting to our feet as the sun became a thin pink rind on the horizon.

"Go over Maeve's for a bit?" Tadhg asked and held out

his hand. "And then home. Or do you need to go to Dublin?"

I took his familiar hand in mine, each callous where I expected it. "No, things in Dublin are grand enough without me. Maeve's for a bit and then home sounds lovely."

This might be a new bliss, I thought. Growing older, towards each other instead of apart. Not an easy path, but still worth giving it a go. And in the long days of summer, the warmth of home and by the sweet song of the sea, it seemed like we'd even have time to walk it.

THE END